DESPERATE MEASURES

A gripping crime thriller filled with twists

CATH STAINCLIFFE

Detective Janine Lewis Book 4

Revised edition 2022
Joffe Books, London
www.joffebooks.com

First published by Allison & Busby Limited
in Great Britain in 2015

This paperback edition was first published
in Great Britain in 2022

Cover art by Nebojša Zorić

ISBN: 978-1-80405-512-0

NOTE TO THE READER

Please note this book is set in the 2000s in England, a time before smartphones, and when social attitudes were very different.

CHAPTER 1

Day One — Tuesday

'No one is killing anyone,' Janine said.

Eleanor and Tom began objecting but Janine raised her hands. 'We finish the meal like civilized human beings, without squabbling or fighting, or you two can go upstairs — no pudding and no screen time.'

'God.' Eleanor made a show of rolling her eyes and Tom scowled.

Charlotte, aged four, clapped her hands.

'That really isn't helping,' Janine said to Charlotte.

Janine seemed to spend half her life as a referee. Eleanor at fifteen was prickly and volatile and dripped misery like every other teenager while Tom, five years her junior, was either winding his sister up or bearing the brunt of her crushing putdowns.

'I want pudding,' Charlotte said.

'Please,' Janine prompted.

'Please.' Charlotte beamed. Happy little soul. Who knows where she'd found that equilibrium. Her life had been the most unsettled to date, born into the immediate aftermath of the marriage break-up, her dad Pete living elsewhere with Tina and now their new baby. Charlotte had been looked after by a succession of nannies with the help of Janine's eldest child Michael while Janine worked. Now Michael had left home, a man of the world, and Janine was still adjusting to the change.

Janine got the ice cream out of the freezer. Running the hot water over a spoon, she caught Eleanor's reflection in the window, mouthing something at Tom. Nothing pleasant, Janine was sure.

'I can see you, Eleanor,' Janine said.

'Well, he's a saddo. I'm sick of it. Loser.' Eleanor lunged forward towards her brother.

'What did I say?' Janine turned round.

I don't want any, anyway,' Eleanor said, 'I hate manky ice cream.' She shoved back her chair and thundered out of the room.

'Hah!' Charlotte said.

'Indeed,' Janine said.

Tom was still brooding, mouth set, brow furrowed.

'You want a flake in it?' Janine said.

'Have we got some?' Tom said.

'We just might have.'

'I couldn't see any,' Tom said.

'Because I have got a new hiding place,' Janine said. If she didn't stash the sweets away the kids attacked them like a plague of locusts.

'You dish this up.' She put the tub of ice cream and the spoon on the table near to Tom.

Out in the hallway, once the door had swung shut behind her, she got the old shopping bag down from the coat rack and picked out three flakes.

She was just helping Charlotte stick one into her ice cream when her phone rang. Richard Mayne, her Detective Inspector.

'You do it.' Janine handed the flake to Charlotte.

'Richard?' Janine moved back into the hall as she answered the call.

'Dead body,' he said, 'just been called in.'

'Suspicious?'

'I'd say — shot three times.'

'OK. I'll see you there.'

Richard gave her the address, on the Chorlton/Whalley Range border, and rang off.

Janine took a breath and went upstairs and knocked on Eleanor's door.

'Go away,' said a muffled voice from inside.

'Eleanor—'

'I don't want any ice cream and I don't want another stupid, boring lecture.'

'I need you to babysit,' Janine said.

A strangled groan from Eleanor.

'I've been called into work,' Janine said.

'I hate your job.'

'Eleanor, I need to go.'

'Why can't you take them to Dad's?' Eleanor said.

'You know why. We've not arranged it and while Alfie's so small it's not fair. You're here and I need you to be responsible.'

'You could ring Sylvie.'

Sylvie was the babysitter cum nanny. 'She's not back till tomorrow,' Janine said. 'I'll pay you.'

Janine was aware of the time, anxious to leave.

'Will you?' A change of tone from Eleanor.

'Yes — and that means I expect you to do it professionally. No being mean to Tom. A bath and bedtime story for Charlotte.'

There was the sound of movement from inside the room. Then Eleanor opened the door. 'How much?' she said.

'The going rate,' Janine said.

'OK.'

'I'll tell them I'm off,' Janine said.

In the kitchen Janine explained about work and stressed to Tom that he had to cooperate with his big sister and no more bickering.

3

'Can I have your ice cream?' he said.

'All right then but not this.' She grabbed the flake and bent to kiss him, he dodged, 'Ewww! Get off.'

Janine kissed Charlotte on the top of her head, less ice cream there than anywhere else, and then set off.

In the car, she keyed the postcode into the satnav and saw that the address was only a couple of miles to the west. It was still light, just before seven, on an early autumn day.

I hate your job, Eleanor had said. And I love it, Janine thought. It was always challenging and there were times when it was exhausting, when it was hard to stomach, times when it could break your heart if you let it. But she was experienced and skilled, she had to be to reach the level of Detective Chief Inspector, and the work was compelling. Most of all, it mattered — to her and her team and to the people who were left behind.

CHAPTER 2

Monday — 24 hours earlier

When the coroner announced the verdict, Adele Young felt as if someone had reached into her chest and torn the heart from her. After all this, the weeks of grieving, the long dark nights with the walls closing in and all she could feel was an absence, Marcie missing, after the battle to try and get someone to listen, to take her seriously and understand that her daughter's death could have been prevented. After all that to be told this.

The clerk was calling for order. Adele's eyes flew across the courtroom to the public gallery where he sat, Dr Halliwell, and she saw relief in the twitch of his mouth, then he looked straight at her, some sort of sick triumph in his eyes.

Accidental death. She staggered and felt Howard grab her, heard him shout, 'Travesty, a bloody travesty!'

Adele bit down hard on her tongue, determined not to weep. She could bawl her eyes out later, in private, but in public she would not give them that satisfaction.

She wondered again how it would've been if Marcie had been some rich white kid instead of a poor black girl. If Marcie had been the GP's daughter or the daughter of the coroner sat up there in his fancy carved chair. Would it have been accidental death then?

People were filing out. She turned to Howard; his eyes burned with outrage.

'The papers will be outside,' she said, 'the telly.' Marcie's inquest had attracted plenty of media attention already. Adele's belief that Dr Halliwell had treated Marcie wrongly and that medical neglect had led to her death made for a human interest story. It had attracted sharks too. Legal firms (at least that's what they called themselves) had hounded her, touting for business, eager to bring suits against the GP. It wasn't money she was interested in, it was recognition, acknowledgment, apology. It was making people see that doctors should listen to their patients, to family and not play God. She didn't want her efforts to be tainted with the smell of chasing money, no matter how hard up they were. And times were hard. Harder than they'd ever been.

'It doesn't stop here,' she said to Howard. 'We carry on.'

He gave a shake of his head. She saw the muscles in his face move, his jaw set tight, too angry to speak. He had been with Adele every step of the way even though Marcie wasn't his by birth. He'd moved in six years back and come to love Adele's daughter as his own. He had been at Adele's side day and night. They'd taken out a loan recently so he could buy a decent suit to wear to the court, and smart shoes. This morning he'd shaved his face and oiled his hair and put on a clean shirt with the suit and she was so proud of him, proud and thankful. He was a fine-looking man, a good man, skin the colour of dark chocolate, almond eyes, a slow smile which still made her stomach turn even after all these years. Not that there had been anything to smile about in these last months.

She put her hand on his shoulder. 'Come on.'

Their appearance outside was stage managed by someone from the court press office. All the main players, the doctor and herself, had to be ready and in place. Adele would be able to speak first, if she wished, then Dr Halliwell. She did wish.

The scrum of photographers and reporters hummed and surged like a swarm of bees.

Adele felt a moment's dizziness and reached for Howard's arm. A microphone was thrust into her face. 'Mrs Young how do you feel about today's verdict?'

'Devastated,' she said with a crack in her voice but she reined in her nerves and spoke louder. 'We are not giving up. We will keep fighting for justice for Marcie until we win.'

'You're not satisfied with the jury's verdict?'

'Satisfied?' Howard shouted, 'This isn't justice, this is a mockery.'

Don't. 'Wait!' She spoke over Howard, squeezing his hand to silence him. If he lost his temper here who knew what he might say or do and then they'd be labelled trouble-makers, lowlife scum, the same as Marcie had been by the worst of gutter press.

She turned back to face the cameras. 'We'll get an independent review for Marcie and if that doesn't work we'll go to the ombudsman. These professionals need to start listening to us, to the families. And we need to stand up for ourselves and for the ones that are vulnerable, like Marcie, because no-one listens to them. We still believe that her care fell well short of what was required. We are especially concerned that our wishes were ignored, our concerns dismissed by her GP and we believe that led directly to her death. If we had been listened to, Marcie would still be with us today.'

Inside her something broke. She felt tears in her throat, and pain in her chest. She fought to breathe. At some signal, a final round of photographs was captured before Adele and Howard were edged away and Dr Halliwell took centre stage. He looked sober, dignified, with his greying hair and his smart camel coat. *Silver spoon*, that's what her mother would've said, *nursed on a silver spoon*.

Dr Halliwell made all the right noises; *Relieved . . . very sad case of Marcie Young . . . sanity prevailed*. As though Adele with her quest was insane, mental, off the wall.

She watched him talk, the man who had been her family GP all her life, who had seen her through her pregnancy and given Marcie her first jabs, the man who prescribed anti-depressants when Adele went to him in tears, at her wit's end with her daughter's antics. The man who, in the last prescriptions he had written for Marcie Young, signed her death warrant as far as Adele was concerned.

She watched him speak, that mock sincerity, slick tongue and clever words. And she hated him. For his arrogance and his lies. For what he had done. She hated him and she wished him dead.

* * *

'You have to keep calm,' Adele said to Howard in the taxi home.

He shot her a glance, his eyes still bright with anger. 'I couldn't believe it,' he said, 'it's all a sham, a fucking sham.'

'It's all there is,' she said.

'People like us, the system is stacked against us.'

'You think I don't know that?' She was suddenly angry at him. 'But there's nothing else we can do.'

He looked away from her, out of the window at the rain. 'He needs teaching a lesson.'

Adele just caught his words. 'Don't you dare,' she said quietly, anxious that the taxi driver might overhear. 'Don't you start thinking like that. That's no answer.'

He didn't reply. They sat in silence. She listened to the beat of the windscreen wipers and the drone of the traffic and closed her eyes. Inside she was trembling, her stomach knotted, her chest aching. She had clung to the hope that today would bring some resolution. Instead they'd been kicked in the teeth.

CHAPTER 3

Monday

Peggy's breathing was worse. Roy checked that the oxygen mask was in the right position and that the cylinder had plenty in reserve.

Peggy was asleep, she'd barely woken in the past few days. The medicine that helped with the pain also made her drowsy.

He wondered if he should send for the priest yet. She was dying. He knew that. Dr Halliwell had explained it clearly, talked to them about hospices, but Peggy wanted to be at home. And Roy wanted her there. Nevertheless calling the priest seemed so final, like throwing in the towel. But if he delayed and she died before having the last rites she'd never forgive him. No, that wasn't true, he thought, Peggy had always been a forgiving sort, a peacemaker, a good Catholic. It was more that Roy would feel bad for letting her down if he misjudged the timing.

She was so young, only sixty, most people lived into their eighties or nineties now. But Peggy had never been strong health-wise: asthma all her life and then the emphysema and the heart trouble, problems to do with her weight, too.

She tried to lose some, countless times, diets and Weight Watchers, eating Ryvita and cottage cheese after making hot pot or pie and chips for Roy. Roy had gained weight too, and more since he stopped work to look after Peggy. At the warehouse he probably used to walk a few miles a day, overseeing the packers, dealing with snarl-ups in the system when incoming stock didn't match the dockets or the goods were faulty.

Now and then, as a young man, he used to go out hiking in the countryside, down to the peaks in Derbyshire. After he met Peggy, walks were gentler, on the level, along riversides or through country parks, the deer park at Dunham Massey, that sort of thing.

Peggy still had a pretty face, round cheeked, warm brown eyes, even though the grey had replaced her chestnut curls.

She stirred a little, made a croaking note as she inhaled, but her eyes didn't open. It was two hours until her next dose was due, though if she woke sooner and asked for it she could have some of the Oramorph. He wouldn't see her suffer. He was clear on that. And the doctor had said there'd be no need.

He'd have to see if she'd take some Movicol as well to help with the constipation. She'd not eaten today. He'd made her Weetabix and warm milk but she couldn't have swallowed more than a teaspoonful.

He left the room quietly and went into the kitchen. The parish bulletin was pinned up on the notice board. Roy took it down and turned it over to read the phone number then keyed it in, ready to speak to Father McDovey.

* * *

Father McDovey put out his hands, took Roy's between them and grasped tightly.

'How are you bearing up?'

'I'm OK,' Roy said, 'thank you, Father. Come through. Would you like a drink?'

'No, thank you,' the priest said, 'I've been plied with tea and biscuits all morning.' He smiled. 'Now.' He set his brief-case down on the kitchen table. 'In here I have an order of service for you, so you can follow what I'm doing.' He drew out a laminated card and passed it to Roy. 'Is Peggy awake?'

'She's drifting in and out,' Roy said, 'but never awake very long now.'

'So Communion?' the priest asked.

'I'm not sure,' Roy said.

'She can swallow?'

'Yes, small amounts.'

'Well, we'll see how it goes. It's a sad time but she has the love of God and his mercy.'

Roy nodded, a lump in his throat.

As the priest began his ministrations, touching Peggy's eyes and nose and mouth with the oil and reciting the prayers for the ceremony, Roy held her hand. He had first met Peggy at church. Roy and Ann, his wife, had separated by then. Roy was still driving the wagon.

During his marriage he'd be away for days at a time, and it got so he dreaded coming home what with Ann complaining about everything, wanting him to be different, to be something he wasn't. He never really understood what she wanted from him. She complained of his silence, his ignoring her, said she wanted holidays, so they went on holidays and then she complained that he was a miserable sod.

'Why did you marry me, then?' he blurted out one day when Ann was having a go.

'I thought I loved you,' she said, 'and I thought you'd change. Wrong on both counts.'

That hurt and she knew it. She looked away and shook her head and said, 'I think it was a mistake, Roy, I'm sorry. I'm just so unhappy.'

So they had parted ways and split the money from the sale of the house. She'd never tried to claim maintenance, at least that was something. Ann moved away, she met a man who was taking over a salon in Alicante and set up with him.

Roy started going to St Agnes's, near his new digs — though his visits were irregular, depending on his schedule. Peggy went too. She got chatting to him one day after mass. Their mothers had known each other, Peggy said. Peggy and he had been to the same primary school, though she'd been three years ahead of him so she would never have noticed him back then.

The next time he saw her, she asked if he'd come with them as a helper for the trip to Lourdes. He was about to refuse, he saw enough of the continent as it was with the truck driving, but the way she smiled changed his mind.

It went on from there, the friendship growing quite slowly, unlike the sudden both-feet-first nature of him and Ann.

After a while he plucked up courage to invite Peggy out for a meal, to an Italian restaurant. He appreciated the company. She would chatter away but it wasn't like the gossip Ann had shared, spiked with putdowns or disapproval. Peggy was more positive than that. She didn't seem to be bothered by his reticence, either. She never chivvied him to talk which made it easier for him to do so.

That evening, outside the house she still shared with her parents, she had kissed him.

'I can't marry you,' Roy said.

'I know,' she said, 'we'll just have to live in sin.'

He stared at her, shocked to the core. He knew how much her faith meant and what it might cost her once word got out.

'It wouldn't be fair,' he said, 'what about church, and your family?'

'It wouldn't be fair if we were kept apart because of some outdated dogma.' Her eyes were warm, merry.

'But people — you know what they're like?'

'Yes. We might have to go to a different church,' she said.

He looked at her — did she mean it, would she really live with him outside of marriage?

'Why should I have to choose between my faith and a chance at happiness?' she said, 'I want both.'

He kissed her then and she responded.

They moved in together a few months later and started going to St Edmund's. Roy bought her a gold ring. Peggy began to use his surname. She had one proviso, she asked if he would consider doing a different job, if he could find something so he wasn't away so much.

He agreed and got the job at the warehouse. He didn't think he could be any happier and then they had Simon.

Now the priest began to recite a Hail Mary. Roy listened, one thumb stroking Peggy's hand, but he didn't join in. He didn't pray anymore. He didn't believe in it.

CHAPTER 4

Monday

'Thank you, Mrs Halliwell.'

'You're welcome, Oliver, tell your mum that I'm very pleased with you. And have a think about the exam will you?'

'Yes, Miss.'

Norma shut the front door. He was a sweet child, polite and good-mannered but natural enough to get the giggles sometimes when he made mistakes that sounded comical. And she laughed along with him. He was her last pupil of the day.

She put the music away in the piano stool, went through and turned the lamp on in the living room and closed the curtains.

An hour later, Don still wasn't back. After all the strain of the inquest and with him completely exonerated she thought he might have come home to relax and well — perhaps celebrate wasn't the right word — but give thanks that the ordeal was over, share that with her. She had made a Boer chicken pie with a beautiful puff top pastry and some cauliflower cheese. It would re-heat in the microwave. She wondered whether to have some herself or to wait and decided that she would have a glass of wine and if he wasn't home by eight then she'd see if she was still hungry.

He had someone else to share his good news with, she was almost certain. That side of things had dwindled between them over time, especially since the menopause. It still happened, but rarely. When they did have sex she wondered why they didn't do it more often. Norma never initiated it, never had, the thought made her toes curl. What if Don said no and turned her away? Sometimes she had dreams and woke aroused, even had an orgasm, but she had never told him.

Norma suspected he had a lover because his hours had got longer again, the partners' meetings more frequent. And she had sensed a new energy to him. At least before the inquest loomed. You don't live with somebody for thirty years without being able to read the smallest changes in mood and behaviour.

There was no point in dwelling on it. There had been other women, other flings. Discreet and short-lived. He would never leave her. She knew this like she knew the scales on the piano keyboard or that the sun would rise in the morning. There was too little loyalty these days, people gave up on marriage at the first hurdle. She was loyal to Don and vice versa.

Norma hadn't attended the Marcie Young inquest. She had offered, dreading that Don might take her up on it, but he'd said, 'I'd only be worrying about you. I'll be fine.'

He wasn't fine though, she had seen the signs of strain on him as the start date drew closer. Last night when he came home, he was ashen-faced, distracted. She teased it out of him, 'How was it, did you have to speak?'

He said a little, then added to it, then elaborated until he was giving full vent to his sense of outrage at the whole charade. He was drinking more, a tumbler of whiskey as soon as he crossed the threshold, wine with his meal. But who was she to comment? He'd been under so much pressure, what with the inquest and problems at the surgery.

Don generally got along with people but one of the GPs, Fraser McKee he was called, got right up Don's nose.

A younger man, he was trying to tell Don how things should be done. He wanted to coach patients and staff to use the Internet, to research current medical thinking, he had ideas for setting up clinics for this, that and the other, as though Don's thirty years in the job counted for nothing.

At first Don had appreciated Fraser's clumsy attempts to innovate, then he began to complain mildly about him, putting it down to the man's inexperience but as the months went on Don became increasingly hostile.

'He's after a partnership,' Don had said, 'he talks as though it's a sure thing.'

'And it's not?' Norma said.

'Over my dead body,' Don had said, 'he's no idea how to work as a member of the team. If you don't agree with his projects and his buzzwords he writes you off.'

'What do the others think?' Norma said.

'He's not made himself popular,' Don said. 'I don't think anyone will disagree.'

* * *

Norma wondered now, as she ironed his shirts, what sort of doctor she herself would have made, if things had turned out differently. Would she have gained the loyalty and affection of her patients and colleagues like Don had or been an irritant like Fraser? Would she even have been a GP? Perhaps she'd have chosen a specialty and gone for a hospital career instead.

At eighteen all she knew was she wanted to study medicine, to save lives. She had worked so hard to get her A levels, to get into medical school, swotting late into the night, taking diet pills to keep awake. Diet pills and black coffee. There were extra classes at school, too, and she went to every one of them. There were about a dozen girls selected for the fast stream, about half of them doing science.

The exams made her terribly anxious, a tightening across her back, churning in her stomach and a clammy sensation across her forehead. She gripped the pen so hard that the indentations remained on her fingers for hours. Once, half way through the first chemistry question, she tore a hole in the paper.

They were in France when the results came out and she had rung Uncle Marty who had opened the letter and read out, 'Four As: biology, chemistry, physics and maths.' Four As! She had her place in Manchester.

The relief was like someone releasing her from an iron lung or something and she'd spent the rest of the holiday having fun with the friends she'd made from the village where the gîte was, in a haze of Gauloises and cheap wine, holiday romance and Pernod.

There were three weeks after they got back from France to get ready for student life. She was going into halls for the first year. She'd never been north and imagined it to be pretty grim but when the training was done she would be able to work pretty much anywhere, even abroad. Doctors were always in demand.

Mummy and Daddy drove her up one fine Saturday afternoon. She felt sick with excitement as they carried clothes and records, her books, sheets and blankets and her castor oil plant up to the room.

Once lectures had started, it didn't take long for that excitement to be replaced with the crushing realization that if swotting for exams had been hard going at school then studying medicine was ten times worse. Until she met Don.

CHAPTER 5

Day 1 — Tuesday

A cordon had been set up to protect the crime scene and the surrounding area. Janine could see the tape, the uniformed officers checking cars and advising residents who needed access.

She could see her sergeants, Shap and Butchers and Lisa, her detective constable talking to the handful of people watching from the opposite pavement. Shap and Butchers looked like a double act, behaved like one often enough. Shap was wiry, sharp and cynical while Butchers was a big man with a belly to match, more of a plodder but meticulous in his police work. Lisa was the one who looked out of place, a striking looking black woman with coffee coloured skin and shiny black curls, she could have been a model, but Janine knew that the young woman was dedicated to the job, keen to learn and make progress.

Janine parked the car and pulled on her protective jumpsuit, collected her mask and gloves and overshoes. It wasn't the most flattering, or the most comfortable outfit, but it was essential if she were to avoid contaminating the scene.

The address was a large detached villa. A notice board by the front wall identified it as a doctor's surgery — and gave the telephone number and opening hours.

Janine showed her ID to the officer guarding the crime scene and ducked under the tape across the driveway entrance.

Ahead she could see the forensics team were already busy. A CSI was taking photographs, documenting the victim and the surroundings. Others were erecting a screen to shield the body. Close by she saw Richard talking to Dr Susan Riley the pathologist and went to join them.

'Susan, Richard,' Janine said.

Richard nodded hello and gestured to the victim. 'Donald Halliwell, sixty-four. General practitioner. The cleaner found him,' Richard said. 'She arrived at half-past six and he was here, like this. Keys just there.'

Janine looked at the man on the ground. Grey-haired, clean-shaven, wearing a charcoal grey suit, his blue striped shirt now soaked with blood from the wounds visible on his chest. He lay just outside the door to the building, his feet, in brown leather brogues, facing the road. A yard away from him were a bunch of keys on a leather fob.

'Did the cleaner touch anything? Go inside?' Janine asked.

'No, called 999 straightaway,' Richard said.

'Cause of death looks fairly obvious,' Susan said. 'We'll be moving him soon and hold a post-mortem tomorrow. A public place like this, we'll be drowning in trace evidence.'

Janine nodded. Other factors might well prove to be more significant as evidence, ballistics on the weapon for example, the doctor's relationships, any motive for someone to kill him.

'The victim's been shot,' Janine said to Richard. 'What's the first thing you think of?'

'Gangs, drugs,' Richard said.

'Exactly,' Janine said. 'But a GP? And in broad daylight? Were there any witnesses?'

'No, not that we know of,' Richard said. 'If anyone did see it happen, you'd think they'd have told us by now. The car's registered to his wife.' Richard gestured across to a car in one of six bays marked *Staff Only* in front of the building. A sign directed patients to a car park at the rear.

'Anything visible in the car? A bag or briefcase?' Janine said.

Richard shook his head. 'No. And no sign of any disturbance inside the building.'

'The door was unlocked?' Janine asked.

'Yes.'

'Was he locking up, perhaps?' Janine said.

'Cleaner says that was often the case, Dr Halliwell would be the last to leave before she arrived. She saw him sometimes. Shall we go in?'

Inside the surgery, there was a reception area to the right and a waiting room to the left. Behind the reception desk were photographs of the practice staff, six in all. Receptionist, practice manager, nurse and three GPs. In his photograph, Donald Halliwell looked fatherly, older than his years, Janine thought. The other two doctors, Anita Gupta and Fraser McKee, were both younger.

They walked on down the broad corridor past four consulting rooms to a bathroom and a locked storage room at the end.

The décor was in good repair, Janine noted, lemon painted walls with green flecked carpeting and white woodwork. Flowers on the reception desk scented the air, paintings hung along the corridor. Richard was right, there was no sign of anything out of place inside the premises.

Back outside, Sergeant Butchers took Janine and Richard to the pavement and introduced them to Ms Ling, the practice manager and key holder. She was a petite woman, of Chinese descent Janine guessed. Her skin was smooth and her face bare of any make-up. She looked young on first impression but Janine saw the fine lines that fanned out from her eyes and the touches of grey in her hair suggesting she was reaching middle age.

'Ms Ling,' Janine said, 'I'm DCI Lewis, I'm in charge of the inquiry. And this is Detective Inspector Mayne.'

Richard said, 'Hello.'

Ms Ling nodded. 'Who would do such a thing?' she said.

'I know,' Janine said, 'I'm sorry. This must be a terrible shock. Have there been any other violent incidents lately? Any threats to Dr Halliwell?'

'No,' Ms Ling said, 'nothing like that.' She blinked fast and her mouth trembled.

'We need to contact the rest of the staff,' Janine said, 'establish if they're safe. Would you be able to help us? If you can give their details to these officers.' She gestured to Lisa, Shap and Butchers.

'Yes of course,' said Ms Ling, 'I'll need to go inside for the files.'

'We can have someone take you round to the fire door at the side,' Janine said.

'Dr Halliwell,' Richard said, 'he would usually carry a bag?'

'Yes, a briefcase,' said Ms Ling.

'What would be in it?' Janine said.

'His prescription pad and first aid kit,' said Ms Ling.

'Any drugs?' said Richard.

'Only small amounts, single doses for emergency use,' Ms Ling said.

'Thank you,' Janine said, 'the surgery will have to remain closed until we have completed our inquiries here.'

'Of course. I'll get the staff details for you,' Ms Ling said.

Janine nodded to Butchers to accompany the manager.

Lisa came over. 'Boss, this is the doctor who was in the news yesterday over the Marcie Young inquest.'

'Really?' Janine, on a rare day off, hadn't caught the news.

'He'll be getting more than his fifteen minutes, then,' said Shap.

Janine glanced at him, always pushing it, was Shap: the cynical comments, the asides and put-downs. He smiled at her. Leave it, Janine thought, pick your battles.

'Marcie Young, that was an overdose, wasn't it?' Janine said.

'Her mother thought the GP was to blame,' Richard said.

'The coroner returned a verdict of misadventure/accidental death,' Lisa said.

'We'll include that in the briefing,' Janine said. At this stage it was impossible to tell what was significant and what was trivia. The only way not to overlook essential details was to collect everything and use systems to collate and cross-reference all the data so it was accessible to the team at a moment's notice.

* * *

A news crew had pitched up and wanted the police to make a statement but Janine had spoken to someone at the Press Office and agreed that no details at all would be released until next of kin had been informed.

Butchers and Shap and Lisa had been contacting other practice staff and now reported back.

'We've spoken to everyone but Fraser McKee, one of the other two GPs, the registrar,' Butchers said. 'He's not answering his phone or his mobile.'

'You take a car over to his house,' Janine said, 'and see if he's there. Shap, Lisa, can you notify next of kin?'

Shap looked pissed off. It was not a job anyone liked doing. He'd probably palm it off on Lisa but then Lisa needed to gain experience in all aspects of the job so that was no bad thing.

Janine watched them go and then walked to her own car. She needed to get back to the station and set all the wheels in motion for the launch of a murder inquiry.

CHAPTER 6

Butchers parked outside the new-build townhouse where
Dr Fraser McKee lived. One of three stuck on the side of
a fenced-off brown site where further development was
planned.

The central house, McKee's was a wreck. The door
hanging off and two windows smashed. He stared for a
moment at the scene of destruction. Then rang into HQ.

'Can we have an area car to 4, Rosedale View, Stretford.
Serious criminal damage to the property, the area is going to
need a forensic exam and the building secured.'

His request logged, he made his way up to the house.
On the threshold he paused and called out, 'Dr McKee? Is
there anyone there? This is the police.' No response. Butchers
couldn't hear any sound from inside the house.

Butchers edged past the lopsided door and into the
open plan living-room and kitchen-diner. The place was a
wreck. Bookshelves had been tipped over, a large TV, its
screen fractured, was on the floor next to a sofa. The sofa
had been slashed and foam stuffing pulled out. A coffee table
lay splintered. It looked like a sledgehammer had been taken
to the place.

The kitchen was similarly ruined: cabinets buckled and broken, appliances (kettle, toaster, coffee-maker) ripped from their sockets and bashed up. Crockery and foodstuffs were strewn about.

Upstairs the destruction continued. Someone, Butchers thought, had been very, very angry. McKee himself — that would account for the fact that he hadn't rung and reported the attack? Or someone else? Had McKee even made it home?

Butchers logged into the database and established what car the GP owned. Then he made a second call. 'Sergeant Butchers, to control. Issue all units to be on the lookout for a grey Peugeot, four zero seven. Registration: mike, alpha, zero, six, foxtrot, mike, delta. And the registered owner, currently missing, Doctor Fraser McKee: white male, late twenties, medium build, dark hair. Thank you.'

Butchers rang the boss next. 'McKee's not home and his car's missing. Someone has done his house over big style. I've put out an obs for McKee and his car. I'll speak to the neighbours now, to see if anyone saw what happened, if they've heard from him.'

Janine turned to Richard. 'The photo of McKee?'

Richard held it up.

'Can we get it copied?' Janine said. 'McKee's car's gone, Butchers says his house is wrecked. Looks like someone's got it in for him. The whole thing just got bigger.'

'Could he be a second victim?' Richard said.

Janine shook her head, it was an appalling prospect.

'Or he's involved?' Richard said.

'And he's demolished his own house to put us off the scent?' Janine said.

Richard shrugged.

If he was the second victim, Janine thought, then who was behind it all? Two GPs targeted. Why? It seemed so bizarre. Some cases, some killings, it was obvious who'd done what and why. Most people knew their killers, most killers left plenty of evidence and it was only a matter of time before they were caught, questioned and charged.

But this? Early days, Janine told herself, the picture would become clearer. The priority now was to find Fraser McKee and hopefully find him safe and well.

* * *

Lisa looked up at Dr Halliwell's home. It was similar to the surgery, perhaps a bit smaller but still a sizable detached house with stained glass windows and black and white trim to the roof. Two lavender shrubs grew in huge urns either side of the door. Piano music could be heard coming from inside. The front garden was laid with paved brick. Everything said des res apart from the car at the far side of the drive which was badly crushed. The driver's side, which was facing them, was caved in, the windows crazed, the front end crumpled. It looked just like someone had forced it against the boundary wall. Lisa glanced at Shap, what on earth was going on?

'That's not a bit of mindless vandalism, is it?' Shap said. 'That's been rammed. It's a total write-off. We've had Halliwell shot, McKee's house damaged, now Halliwell's car. . .'

They walked up to the door and Shap knocked.

The music carried on and a woman opened the door. She was thin with ash-blonde hair, and was dressed in a pleated navy skirt and powder blue blouse, pearls at her neck and in her ears. A classic look, Lisa thought, timeless. The sort of thing you could get in the boring bits at M&S if you wanted. Never go out of fashion. Never in fashion either, as far as Lisa was concerned.

'Mrs Halliwell? Norma?'

'Yes.'

'I'm DC Goodall,' Lisa said, 'and this is Sergeant Shap, may we come in?'

The woman gave a frown. 'They told Don they'd send someone tomorrow.'

What's she on about, Lisa wondered, crossed wires somewhere?

25

Norma Halliwell showed them into the hallway, black and white tiles on the floor, polished wood banisters and thick cream carpets on the stairs. Cream, thought Lisa, how did they keep them clean?

'Will it take long?' Norma Halliwell said, 'Only I have a pupil.' She gestured to the front room where the piano music was playing.

'Perhaps you could ask them to leave?' Lisa said.

Norma Halliwell made a little sound of surprise.

'It could take a while,' Lisa said.

For a moment it looked like she might argue the toss about it but then the woman said, 'Very well.' She disappeared into the room. The music stopped.

'Have you got the tissues?' Shap said, winding Lisa up. He'd know she was nervous, this the first time she'd given the death message. The sarky comments were maybe his way of trying to help — but they didn't.

Norma Halliwell came out with a young lad and saw him to the door. 'Bye bye, Jordan, see you next week, we'll make up the time then.'

She closed the door and turned to Shap and Lisa. 'Please, come in.'

The front room was spacious and well-furnished with a piano and paintings and tapestries on the walls.

'Please sit down, Mrs Halliwell,' Lisa said.

Norma Halliwell sat on one of the winged armchairs. She looked bemused, almost smiling, as though this might be some weird game they were playing.

Lisa's chest felt tight and her face warm as she said, 'We have some very bad news, I'm sorry to have to tell you that your husband, Dr Halliwell, has been the victim of a violent attack.'

'He's been hurt?' Norma Halliwell looked stunned, her mouth hung open.

'I'm sorry,' Lisa said, 'he's dead.'

There was a beat, a little snort of disbelief from Norma Halliwell who frowned and shook her head quickly and said, 'Sorry?' as though she might have misheard.

'Dr Halliwell is dead,' Lisa said. She knew it sounded brutal but it was important to be clear, to leave no room for doubt.

'Oh, no. Please, no,' she said, 'but how? What happened?'

'He was found outside the surgery,' Lisa said, 'he appears to have been shot.'

'Shot?' Norma Halliwell seemed completely dazed. Lisa didn't know how much time they'd have while the woman could still string two words together.

'Mrs Halliwell?' Lisa said, 'Can you tell us when you last saw your husband?'

'Erm, when he left for work, this morning. About, erm, quarter past eight,' she said.

'He took your car?' Shap said.

'Oh, yes. His . . . well, you've seen it?' Norma Halliwell said. 'I thought that's why you were here.'

'What happened to his car?' Shap said.

'We were asleep, last night, there was this almighty crash, terrible noise, then another and the sound of a car screeching away.' Her voice shook. 'Don went to look and someone had just driven right into it. Deliberately.'

'Do you know who?' Shap said.

Norma Halliwell shook her head.

'Can you think of anyone who would wish him harm?' Lisa said.

Norma Halliwell began to cry, covered her nose and mouth with her hands. 'No,' she sobbed.

'Did your husband own a gun?' Shap said.

'A gun? No.'

'I'm very sorry to ask you this but we will need someone to make a formal identification once the post-mortem has been completed. Probably later tomorrow,' Lisa said.

'No!' Norma Halliwell gasped. 'I can't. I can't do that. Don't make me.'

'Of course not,' Lisa said. 'I'm sure one of Mr Halliwell's colleagues will be able to do it but we always ask next of kin first.'

'I'm sorry,' the woman said, tears on her face, 'I just can't.'

Lisa try to persuade Mrs. Halliwell to contact someone, a friend or relative or neighbour to come and sit with her but she steadfastly refused. It felt awkward, cruel, leaving her alone after dropping such a bombshell but Lisa couldn't force the woman against her wishes.

Outside Lisa looked again at the damaged car. 'If the same person as shot him did that,' she said, pointing to the car, 'then we might be able to find material from the culprit, or at least his vehicle, here and at the crime scene.'

'Not a bad idea,' Shap said. He got out his phone and selected a number. 'We want a forensic exam on the victim's car,' he said, 'which is currently at the home address. Full lift of the vehicle to the garage then cross reference and see if there's any evidence linking this to the murder crime scene.'

CHAPTER 7

Norma lay on the bed. She wanted to turn over and open her eyes, to see Don there, solid, real. To make that real, not this. Not this appalling thing they had told her. Forty-four years together and now she was alone. She would snap under the pressure, that her bones would crack like twigs and her head burst and her heart collapse. She had heard the adage that a woman had to be twice as good as a man to do half as well and here it was writ large. The lecturers, from the most junior to the professors, treated her in one of two ways: either she was invisible, ignored when tasks were allocated or opinions invited; or she was a dolly-bird for them to leer at or fondle. The first time her anatomy tutor slapped her bottom she felt a rush of shame followed by a sting of anger but all she did was giggle like some character in a Carry On film. And on the rare occasion that Professor Malkin spoke to her, he stared at her breasts all the while. She hated it but had to put up with it. She'd have been blacklisted if she'd tried to object or complain.

By the summer term of the first year she was close to dropping out. No matter how hard she studied, how many hours she spent reading in the library or memorizing schema and lists until the words danced and blurred on the page and her neck was locked stiff and her headache grew more nauseating, she was never more than mediocre in her tests and essays. She feared she would not get through her exams.

It was then, at her lowest point, that she first met Don. She was on campus, unlocking her bike ready to go home. It was windy and her hair was whipping in her eyes. She climbed onto the seat, pedalled a few yards and felt a jarring sensation. A puncture. She burst into tears, feet planted either side of the bike, hands covering her eyes. Then she heard him. 'Give it a good kicking. That's what I do.'

She didn't know him, he wasn't in her intake. She sniffed, wiped her face. Said nothing.

'Or maybe not in those.'

Her shoes were open-toed. She wore flatties for rounds but kept decent shoes in her locker.

'I can offer you coffee?' he said.

She was about to refuse, not knowing if he would expect something in return.

'Or bus fare home?'

'I've got bus fare,' she said.

'Coffee then. Come on, it's bloody freezing.'

She went with him, wheeling her bike, to the Italian coffee bar around the corner.

'I'm Don,' he said, on the way, 'third-year medicine.'

'Norma,' she said, wondering if her mascara had run. 'First year, but probably not for much longer.' She meant to make a joke of it but it sounded like she was whining so she added, 'Sorry, awful day . . . week.'

'I could tell you it'll get easier,' he said, holding the café door open for her, 'but I'd be lying.'

She groaned.

Settled with their espressos, he offered her a cigarette. She took it, grateful to have something to fiddle with, she felt so awkward.

He chatted away, making her laugh with his comments on the teaching staff. He seemed so confident, not at all ill at ease given he'd just seen her bawling her eyes out. He just seemed to believe everything was basically all right.

His company, the cigarette and the coffee, the warm fug of the place helped her to relax so that when he finally said, 'So what's the hardest thing?' she could answer without welling up. 'I can't sleep,' she said. 'It just keeps going round and round and then I'm simply exhausted. And I get these blinding headaches. I've tried Pro Plus but I can't see that it's helping.'

'You need a doctor.' He smiled. He'd thick fair hair, just touching his collar, a slightly ruddy complexion like someone who enjoyed the outdoors. A hearty look. He didn't walk her home but he did invite her to the pictures the following week. And when they met he brought with him something she could use for the headaches and something for sleeping.

Those heady days when they were first in love, when they couldn't keep their hands off each other. She'd tried the birth control pill but the side effects, the bloated feeling, the tension and PMT were dreadful. At the family planning clinic they said she could use a different brand or the Dutch cap but she thought that was just too messy, and she didn't want to stop each time and put it in, so eventually she opted for a coil. It would allow her to be spontaneous, just as the pill had, to respond whenever he reached for her.

She passed her exams, just, and made it through to the second year and she'd moved into a room in Don's shared house. It was a way of living together without upsetting their parents.

Don was right, medical school had not got any easier, but the painkillers sorted out her headaches and she was sleeping better, she was less anxious. Sometimes it was still hard to concentrate but she didn't get all in a state about it. They were both working flat out but there were always uppers available if they needed a kickstart for a party at the end of a long week.

Don had the constitution of an ox, no matter how much he drank or what he took, he'd wolf down a full English breakfast and coffee and aspirin and be ready for anything. Norma couldn't stomach food on those mornings, she would take more tablets and drink some water and do her best to sleep the day away. If she did try and face the world she felt queasy and shaken as though some terrible thing had happened and she was partly to blame. It fuelled her anxiety so it was best to hide away. She would emerge at teatime, finally ready for a plate of macaroni cheese or liver and onions or whatever Don had thrown together. Usually Norma cooked, her mother had taught her, though it was important to make things she could do quickly with the burden of work still so heavy. And they could only afford cheap cuts. Don had a full grant, Norma's parents gave her a modest allowance and they tried to live within their means.

Don was very protective of her. When one of the other housemates, a boy from Liverpool, referred to her as 'the Duchess' on account of her accent and the fact that her family were comfortably off, Don had said, 'Her name is Norma.' And his tone was so cold and firm that Robbie, who could be quite argumentative, simply held up his hands and muttered, 'Fine by me, kiddo.'

There was a photograph she remembered from that time. Don's 21st. Most people celebrated their 18th by that time and Don had done, at home, but he wanted to celebrate this time, just with friends. They had a house party. Someone's girlfriend took a photo early on. Robbie made some punch, which had Norma squiffy after one glass. The housemates posed in the back garden, Norma in the centre, Don and Robbie either side of her and the other two girls on either edge. Norma looked like a doll next to Don, pale even though it was summertime. She never could take the sun, went red and peeled if she tried to. Her hair was silver blonde, her head reached his chest. She sometimes wondered if Don's desire to support and defend her came from the fact that she was so petite. If he had been shorter or she'd been taller or less slender would he still have treated her like that? Or would he have done that for anyone he loved?

And now — where was he now? How could he just leave her like this? How would she survive? Norma felt despicable, the shame hot in her guts because when the police told her he was dead, her first thought was not for Don — she didn't think about what might have happened to him or if he had suffered — but for herself. What it meant for her. She was so selfish. But how would she cope without him? It was impossible. She pushed the thought away and went in search of solace. Something medicinal, she thought, tears standing in her eyes, for the shock.

For the shock.

CHAPTER 8

It had all seemed to happen so quickly, she thought, as Adele went over and over the sequence of events during the day after the inquest: Marcie changing from a goofy twelve-year-old who liked baking and *Buffy the Vampire Slayer* and hanging around the Arndale Centre with her mates from school, to a sulky, withdrawn girl who was out all hours and bunking off.

It was Howard who first called it. Adele thought it was teenage rebellion (and maybe that was part of it) and that after a few months of back-chat and door slamming and sleepless nights for Adele, Marcie would re-emerge but as soon as money started disappearing from his wallet and Adele's purse Howard realized. 'She's using it for drugs,' he said.

'No way. She'd never touch them, she doesn't even smoke,' said Adele, who couldn't kick her own fifteen-a-day habit. 'You're wrong.'

They'd confronted Marcie who had sworn on her grandma's grave that she'd never touched any drugs or taken any money and had flounced out of the house.

Adele was wild with anxiety. She looked up help lines and advice services, all the while thinking maybe Howard was mistaken. Then the police came round. Marcie had been caught breaking into a car.

It was all downhill after that.

Those endless nights, lying awake, Adele kept imagining her hurt or being hurt, nodding off in some filthy rat hole or freezing to death in a shop doorway. Some nights they'd go out looking for her, driving around, a blanket and a thermos for her in the back.

They found her a couple of times and persuaded her to come home. And the next time Marcie left, something else would be missing, jewellery, mobile phone, DVDs — anything portable she could sell.

The hardest thing was Marcie's point blank refusal to talk about what was happening, to admit that was a problem, to accept that she was an addict. Smelling dirty and with her face all spots and scabs, she'd eat sugar by the spoonful, half a bag at a time. She was skin and bone in a few short months. There was sometimes a moment when Adele caught sight of the girl beneath all this, a glint of mischief in her gaze, but most of the time the habit seemed to swallow Marcie whole.

Adele was frantic to help but could see no way. If she'd had more money she could've paid for the stuff herself, rationing it out, so at least the stealing and lying and run-ins with the police wouldn't happen.

The spectre of prostitution hovered close by. Adele didn't know if Marcie was already embroiled in that but knew that it came with the territory. Prostitution, AIDS, homelessness, overdoses.

Don't give them money, that was what all the charities said, money will go straight to the addiction. It doesn't help. Not the answer.

'What's it like?' Adele asked her one evening. Marcie was getting jittery. Adele could see it in the way her eyes swung about, the muscles jumping under her skin. 'What does it feel like, the heroin?'

Marcie waited a moment, mouth open, finding the words, then said, 'Heaven.' And a look of lust and longing filled her eyes.

'What it does to you, what it's doing . . .'

Marcie shivered and scratched her neck. 'You don't get it,' she said.

'Maybe not,' Adele said, her voice rising, 'but what I do get is that you can't carry on like this, babe. It'll kill you. Don't go out,' she had begged later, 'I'll sit up with you.'

The next time Howard had seen Marcie on his way home from work, begging. The building was in a row that had been waiting years for redevelopment. Boards over the windows, grass in the guttering, pigeons on the roof. The place was freezing cold, the stones glistening damp, a smell of wet earth and human mess. Marcie was filthy, dirt ingrained in her hands, pin thin arms livid with sores and needle marks.

Adele had thought that was the lowest point. To see Marcie had started injecting now, that the high couldn't come fast enough or go deep enough.

They had brought her home, stuck her in the shower, given her clean clothes, fed her Coco Pops and toast and drinking chocolate. Adele slept with her purse under the pillow. Twelve hours later Marcie had gone again.

* * *

The turning point had been an intervention from a drug abuse officer who worked with the neighbourhood policing team. Marcie had been arrested again and was facing possible charges which could lead to a custodial sentence. The officer, Sandra Gull, was working with a small group of offenders with substance abuse issues to try and get them on the rehab route. Faced with the choice, Marcie agreed to try the scheme. The day Marcie went to the surgery to see Dr Halliwell about the methadone replacement programme, Adele felt as though the sun had returned after a long, dark, winter. Hope replaced dread. Sandra was having excellent results with the programme and lives were being saved. Adele felt hopeful, at least for those first few weeks before it all went so very wrong.

CHAPTER 9

Fraser McKee's neighbours on one side were away, according to the ones on the other side, who were only just arriving back from work as Butchers went to greet them and were astonished to see the state of the house. So the police had no witnesses to the destruction of the property.

Butchers was heading for the police station when he was notified that there'd been a road traffic accident involving Fraser McKee's Peugeot on the dual carriageway near the airport car-hire village in Wythenshawe.

Butchers doubled back and made his way there.

His first thought, as he saw the car, was that they'd got a second fatality. The vehicle was upside down, on its roof, on the grass verge, at a bend in the road. A traffic police unit was attending.

One of the traffic officers came to meet him and Butchers introduced himself, explained they were looking for McKee. The officer told Butchers the Peugeot was empty and there was no sign of any occupants in the immediate vicinity.

Butchers looked up the road, 'Any cameras?'

'No. Not on this stretch.'

'Can I take a look?' Butchers asked.

'Sure. We've got blood on the driver's side. The driver is likely to be injured.'

Butchers crouched down to peer into the vehicle. The airbag had inflated and there were smears of red on that, more on the side window.

'Could he have walked away?' Butchers asked.

'See all sorts,' the traffic officer replied.

Butchers rang and discussed the situation with the boss. She agreed he could organize a search of the immediate area but not to run it all night, give it a couple of hours then close it down.

* * *

It was close to midnight when Janine arrived home. She sat for a moment in the car, summoning the energy to move. Her back ached and her feet throbbed, she felt light headed and slightly nauseous from too many cups of coffee and not enough to eat.

It was quiet as she got out of the car, just the sound of a goods train rattling through the station, almost a mile away.

It had been a long day. Tonight Don Halliwell's widow was facing a future on her own, her world torn apart by the violent death of her husband.

And Fraser McKee?

Whoever was after McKee meant business, Janine thought to herself. And, if they had caught up to him, Janine and her team could be faced with investigating a double murder.

All Janine wanted to do was sleep.

The kitchen looked more or less how she'd left it, the dirty dishes still on the table, though someone had put the ice cream away — unless they'd polished it off. Janine surveyed the mess, considered leaving it till morning but told herself to just stop wimping out and get on with it.

Half an hour later, after checking Tom and Charlotte were safe in their beds, she got into her own, setting the alarm for six-thirty and praying that Charlotte wouldn't wake in the night.

* * *

The constable on the front desk looked up as the buzzer sounded for the exterior door. The security lamp illuminated the man outside: youngish, suit and tie, short sandy-coloured hair, face cut and bruised, blood stains on his shirt collar. A fight, the constable wondered, or a drunk? Or both? He wasn't a regular customer. There was no match on tonight. Tuesdays were usually quiet. The man's body language wasn't aggressive, he wasn't mouthing off or hammering to get in, so the constable released the door switch.

The man limped up to the counter, his face pale, his breath coming fast as though he'd been running. 'You've got to help me,' he said, 'I need protection. My name's Dr Fraser McKee and somebody's trying to kill me.'

CHAPTER 10

Day Two — Wednesday

As soon as Janine heard that Fraser McKee was in police custody for his own protection, she arranged to have him transferred to her station for interview as a victim and potential witness.

Her first impression was that the man was scared witless, tension evident in the set of his shoulders, the light in his eyes. Wounds on his face had been cleaned up but Janine doubted that he'd got any sleep.

'I'm DCI Janine Lewis,' she told him, 'in charge of the inquiry into the murder of Dr Halliwell.'

McKee nodded, rubbed a finger under his nose.

'DI Richard Mayne,' Richard introduced himself.

'You've seen a doctor,' Janine said. 'Is there anything else you need?'

'No.' McKee kept blinking, pale lashes against pale blue eyes. He seemed to find it hard to maintain eye contact.

'Perhaps you could tell us what happened?' Janine said.

'I . . . erm . . .' he was jittery, a fist tapping on the edge of the table as he talked, 'I left work and went home and my house . . . they'd completely wrecked it. It was . . . it was incredible, the scale of the destruction. I knew what it meant — they were after me. I had to get away, so I . . . erm, I got in the car and started driving. I didn't know where to go. They'd be looking for me.' His breath was uneven, panicked.

Janine wondered who 'they' were but didn't want to break the flow yet. She nodded for him to continue.

'Then the news about Don came on the radio. They'd killed Don, oh God, and now my house and I didn't know what to do.' He splayed his hands, imploring. 'Then this car was right up behind me, he forced me off the road. My car turned over, I thought I'd had it . . . I got out and I just ran, there were woods nearby and I hid there for a while until it got dark, then I made my way to the police station.' He stopped, his breath uneven and noisy in the small room.

'What time was it when you left work?' Janine said.

'About five thirty,' McKee said.

'Dr Halliwell was still there?' Janine said.

'Yes.'

'You sound as though you know who's behind all this,' she said.

McKee hesitated, his eyes intense, then said, 'It's the Wilson Crew, you've heard of them? They broke into the surgery before and now they've come back and Don's got in their way.'

The Wilson Crew were notorious, one of several Manchester gangs who made money primarily from drug pushing and robberies and maintained their power by intimidating anyone who they perceived to be a threat. Gangs were responsible for the majority of shootings in the city. The police operation Xcalibre had been set up to try and purge them from the city streets.

'No-one was convicted for the previous break-in,' Janine said.

'But everyone knew it was them, and stuff like this: shooting, the state of my house, who else could it be?' His voice was high with fear.

Janine couldn't make sense of what he was saying. 'Dr McKee,' she said, 'if we accept for a moment that Don Halliwell was shot because he interrupted an attempted break-in, I don't see why these same people would then set out to vandalise your property and threaten your life.'

He looked incredulous. 'Because they can, because that's how they work isn't it? They intimidate people.' As an explanation it didn't hold water.

Richard shifted in his seat. Janine could tell he wasn't convinced either.

'What can you tell us about the vehicle that ran you off the road?' Richard said.

'It was dark, some sort of 4x4, with those blacked-out windows,' McKee said.

'Could you see how many people were in it?' Richard said.

McKee shook his head.

'Was there any actual impact? It might help us with forensics,' Richard said.

'I'm not sure. I was just trying to get away, it all happened so fast.' McKee swallowed, rubbed at his nose again.

'Was the road busy?' Richard said. He was wondering about witnesses, Janine thought.

'No,' McKee said.

'And the other car didn't stop?' Richard said.

'I don't know. I think I was unconscious but I don't know how long for,' McKee said.

Janine leant forward, 'Have there been any threats made in the past to you or to other staff by these people?' she said.

'No,' said McKee.

'And they're not personally known to you?' Janine said.

'No,' McKee said, his eyes darting away.

Janine asked him if he'd be happy to wait as they made further inquiries and would want to talk to him again.

'I can stay here?' he said.

'Yes,' she said and he gave a nod.

'What do you think?' Janine said to Richard as they travelled up in the lift.

'His story's a bit of a dog's dinner,' Richard said.

'Yes. I'm not sure he was being straight with us,' she said.

'In fear for his life,' Richard said.

'Yes, I believe that but he seemed paranoid. All that stuff about the Wilson Crew targeting him just because they can. I don't buy that.'

'Do you think he knows something about the murder?' Richard said.

'I can't tell but he's holding something back, something that scares him enough to bring him here,' Janine said.

CHAPTER 11

Once the reference to the Wilson Crew had been entered into the inquiry log and before she could brief the team, Janine was contacted by DCS Roper from Xcalibre, the gun crime operation. Roper wanted to know where her interest in the Wilsons stemmed from. After she'd explained, he invited himself over to the briefing. Her inquiry had blundered into Xcalibre territory and Roper sounded hell-bent on making it clear where they could and couldn't tread. 'Sounds like it does involve the gang,' Janine said to Richard, 'at least something's becoming clearer.'

* * *

Janine waited for Roper to arrive and took him into the incident room where the team were assembled. The boards contained significant information so far on all lines of inquiry: a picture of Halliwell and his details in the centre with a section on the crime scene, including a note about the missing briefcase and weapon, and a section on Norma Halliwell and the vandalised car, and a map of the area near the surgery. To the left, the team had compiled details of the practice, a list of colleagues and a section on McKee with pictures of his house and the crashed Peugeot. To the right, the new line of inquiry into the gangs, the Wilson Crew and the previous robbery.

'Some of you may know DCS Roper, from Xcalibre, our gun crime operation,' Janine said, 'he has an interest in our current case as you'll hear.'

Roper nodded and took the floor. 'Good morning. I'm here because the Wilson Crew were flagged up to us as of interest to your investigation and what I can tell you is that at present we have the inner-circle, the half-dozen people at the top, under close surveillance. We do know there was talk of another burglary but no immediate plans to carry it out. We can confirm that members of the gang were party to the property damage to Fraser McKee's house yesterday but we can also confirm that the murder of Dr Halliwell was not instigated or carried out by those we are monitoring.'

Janine saw the ripple of surprise travel round the room. Shared it herself. The proximity of the incidents, the connection between Halliwell and McKee had persuaded her, persuaded all of them, that the crimes were linked by the same perpetrators but Roper was saying that categorically was not the case.

'What about the attack on Halliwell's car?' Shap said.

'And McKee's?' Butchers said.

'No, neither of those incidents are linked to the Wilson Crew,' said DCS Roper.

'Do you know why they ransacked McKee's place?' Richard said.

'Not yet. What I should make clear is that just because we rule out the top-dogs for commissioning or carrying out the shooting, it could still be a gang member. The gang structure is pretty fluid, there might be eighty people or more loosely affiliated at any one time. Some are related to the big boys, others just live in the area, run the odd errand.'

'It could be the work of a splinter group,' Janine said.

'Possibly. They tend to be the younger ones, who can often be more reckless, more violent,' Roper said. 'But we

haven't had any intelligence through on that. It's just specu-
lation. All I can say is this killing was not sanctioned by the
gang leadership.'

'It's an unusual target,' Janine said, 'middle-aged GP.'

'I'll grant you that,' Roper said, 'gang violence tends to
arise from gang activity, rival groups vying for control, fall-
ings out within the gang. Sometimes it spills over to friends
and relatives, then of course we get mistaken identity, that
sort of shooting. But this. . .' He shook his head. 'If I were
putting money on it I'd say this was not a gang related killing.'

'Not even some rogue scrote on the edge of the action?'
Shap said.

Roper shrugged. He paused for a minute then said,
'Obviously we don't want to blow our obs . . .'

'You don't want us pulling in your suspects,' Richard
said.

'And there's no need,' DCS Roper said, 'the leaders
are clear for the murder, and no-one wants to see eighteen
months of work go down the drain picking them up for
criminal damage to the McKee property. If your continuing
inquiries lead you to conclude any involvement from any
wider associates I'd appreciate being kept up to speed.'

'Understood,' Janine said.

Once Roper had left, Janine led the discussion, 'So the
Wilson Crew trashed McKee's house but someone else drove
him off the road. He's a popular guy.'

'Like Lancelot said,' Shap chipped in, 'could be an off-
shoot gang.'

'The last burglary,' Butchers said, 'the intruders got away
with a load of computers and prescription pads. The alarm
went off but by the time an area car responded they'd legged it.'

'And was there any evidence to link it to the Wilson
Crew at the time?' Janine said.

'No, only hearsay,' Butchers said.

'Suppose it was a splinter gang, a copycat crime,' Lisa
said, 'this time they go in at the end of the day but Halliwell
confronts them and they shoot him.'

'OK,' said Janine, 'investigating that is one priority. The other is Halliwell's workplace. After all, that's where he was shot. We need to build up a picture of Dr Halliwell. What can the rest of the staff tell us? We're talking to them this morning. But we also look at patients.'

'Place like that you get all sorts,' Shap said, 'nutters, junkies.'

'Sick people,' Janine said. 'You not have a doctor, Shap?'

'Nah,' Shap said.

'No-one to check your bits?' Janine said.

'Don't need a doctor for that,' Shap said, 'they're lining up for it.'

Lisa groaned and Butchers laughed.

'Queasy,' Janine said, 'spare us.'

'How about a patient with a grudge?' Richard said. 'They do Halliwell's car, then the shooting.'

'Needs exploring,' Janine agreed. 'Lisa, you mentioned the Marcie Young inquest.'

'Yes, boss. Dr Halliwell was cleared of any negligence and the verdict was accidental death.'

'How did the family take it?' Janine said. 'See what you can find out.'

'Will do,' Lisa said.

'Other actions?' said Janine.

'We've pulled in CCTV for the area,' Lisa said, 'and we're looking for activity near the scene: people, cars. Same with house-to-house.'

'We're also working back through his day,' Butchers said, 'getting the timeline filled in.'

'Good,' Janine said, 'We've arranged to talk to staff at the surgery now, and I intend to speak to Dr McKee again after that. And attend the post-mortem. We'll review everything at five-thirty.'

CHAPTER 12

Roy was no stranger to organizing funerals. He'd helped with his father's, sorted out his mother's, then Peggy's parents and —

He was startled by a blare from the horn of the car behind him. The lights had changed to green and Roy sat there like an idiot. He drove on. He had the death certificate now from the registrar. The registrar had offered to print out extra copies in case he needed to send them to Peggy's bank or building society or anywhere else but Roy had declined. They had a joint account, the house was rented, he wouldn't need them.

Cooper's, a Catholic firm were doing the funeral, there'd been an opening at the cemetery on Saturday afternoon. There was no need to wait any longer — it wasn't as if there were any family who needed time to travel. It'd be Roy and Peggy's friends, most of them from church. Father McDovey would do a Requiem Mass at St Edmund's beforehand.

Roy pulled into the road at the side of the surgery. The place was closed. He had watched the news this morning, reports that someone had been shot. Later they named the victim as Dr Donald Halliwell. The main entrance was taped off but Roy could see the fire door at the side was open and a police officer stood there. He parked and lifted the tank out and walked along the path to her.

'Surgery's closed,' she said.

'I'm just returning this,' Roy said, 'it won't take a minute.' He had already rung up to arrange the return of the hospital bed and they would collect on Friday.

'If you could come back tomorrow,' the officer said.

Roy felt a flash of anger, hot across his back. My wife's just died, he wanted to tell her, she spent the last weeks of her life hooked up to that thing and I want rid of it. Now.

He said nothing, then he caught sight of Miss Ling behind, in the hallway.

'Roy,' she said, 'come in.' The police officer glared at him but stood to one side. 'I heard about Peggy,' Ms Ling said. 'I am so sorry.

'And Dr Halliwell,' he said.

'It's awful. Unbelievable.' She had been crying.

'I just wanted to drop the oxygen off,' he said, 'but then—'

'Of course.' She glanced sharply at the officer. 'No problem.'

The policewoman tightened her lips and he wished he had the nerve to challenge her attitude but what if he lost his temper and caused a scene when they were trying to work out what happened to the doctor?

So he said nothing but left the cylinder where Ms Ling showed him. He could see other people in the building, a woman who looked at him as he came in. And a tall man near the consulting rooms. They weren't in uniforms but he got the impression they were police too. Ms Ling asked when the funeral was and she said she'd try and come and that made him feel a bit better.

On the drive home he remembered going to the surgery with Peggy for the results of the tests; how they had sat side by side while Dr Halliwell told them that it was bad news, that the shadow was a tumour on the lung and that it was unfortunately very advanced.

'How advanced?' Peggy had said.

'But can you treat it?' Roy said at the same time.

'The only treatment will be palliative,' Dr Halliwell said, 'to make you comfortable. I am sorry.'

Sorry, he had said but it wasn't his fault, was it? The luck of the draw. Terminal, Roy thought. The word hadn't been spoken but that's what it was. Terminal.

There was a rushing in his head and he felt sick. He clamped his jaw tight.

'How long have I got?' Peggy had said.

'Impossible to say.' Dr Halliwell shook his head.

'Roughly?'

'Peggy,' the doctor reproached her.

'Please, doctor, you must have some idea. Months? A year?'

Dr Halliwell took a breath, his fingers on the knot of his tie.

Weeks, then, Roy thought.

'A year would be most unlikely,' the doctor had said

'Thank you,' Peggy said.

For what? A death sentence? Roy was furious. How could she be so accepting? Why wasn't she full of rage at the unfairness of it all? She deserved better. God knows, she'd been through enough in the past few years.

Roy had got abruptly to his feet and let go of her hand. He had to leave.

Dr Halliwell looked up at him and said to them both, 'It's an awful lot to take in. Why don't you go home and I'll call in tomorrow afternoon and we'll look at your care plan then.'

Care plan? How had it come to that? One minute she was a bit more breathless, had a pain in the side, next thing she was dying and had a care plan.

Peggy stood up. 'Yes, thank you, doctor,' she said again. Roy followed her out, the injustice of it a searing fire in his chest.

And it had been weeks. Five short weeks from that day until her death yesterday.

Dr Halliwell had called just after lunch.

Roy had been up with Peggy all night, dozing in the armchair, beside the big hospital bed. He'd had to move furniture out of the room to accommodate it but there was just enough space for the chair and the small table to put all the medicines and things on.

When it grew light, Roy had made a cup of tea. He'd asked Peggy if she'd like a drink of anything but she didn't wake. Her breath was irregular even with the oxygen and several times she made a gargling sound. Roy worried she was choking at first, he sprang up and watched, ready to try and clear her throat if he had to but then he saw the ripple in her throat as she managed to swallow and he sat back down again, took hold of her hand.

He didn't speak. There was no need for words. Now and again a noise from outside would pierce his consciousness: the slam of a car door, a burst of bird song, a plane overhead; but in the cocoon of the room, over-warm for Peggy, he let his mind drift.

Peggy began to cough and then her breath made a stuttering, scraping sound. He felt her hand slacken. And then there were no more breaths. Roy waited a while to be sure, an awful aching in his throat. He rubbed his eyes and he gently removed the oxygen mask and smoothed her hair back. He folded her hands on her chest and gazed at her for a few more minutes before calling the surgery.

Dr Halliwell gave his condolences when he arrived in the early afternoon. He said he'd finished his home calls and thought it was best to visit Roy last so he could take as much time as they needed. Roy offered him tea but the doctor said he was popping home after this. He explained that, as Peggy's death was expected, Roy was free to call the undertaker and could take the doctor's death certificate to the registry office.

'She was at home with you, where she wanted to be,' Dr Halliwell said.

Roy gave a nod.

'It will get easier, life goes on,' the GP said.

Roy bit his cheek, didn't trust himself to answer. He took the piece of paper from the doctor and put it on the arm of the chair.

'There'll be a lot to sort out now, with all the arrangements,' Dr Halliwell said. 'It'll keep you busy. But you may find things a bit harder after that, with time on your hands. Any problems sleeping, anything like that, do come and see me. Now I'll leave you to it unless there's anything else?' He spread his hands.

Roy shook his head.

Once Dr Halliwell had gone, Roy picked up the death certificate, his hands shaking, the paper trembling and the words shivering on the page.

Roy pulled up outside the house and parked.

Inside, the curtains were still closed, the place cold. He had turned the heating off. He sat in the chair in the room and closed his eyes and imagined Peggy's hand in his.

CHAPTER 13

The police tape remained in place. A laminated A4 notice on the gate post explained the surgery was closed. Inside, the phone was ringing, over and over again, cutting off each time as the answer machine kicked in.

The staff were assembled in the waiting room. There was a hushed, shocked atmosphere. Ms Ling sat with a pile of folders on her knees, face drawn. Beside her was the receptionist Vicky Stonnall, young, plump with her head dyed an improbable shiny purple and sporting oversized rings and a golden necklace like a mayoral chain. Opposite them were Dr Gupta and the practice nurse. The doctor wore black-rimmed glasses perched half way down her nose, her hair salt and pepper. Janine judged her to be in her 40s. Nurse Dawn Langan had been crying, nose pink at the end, and had a balled up tissue in her hand. Her blonde hair was pulled back into a ponytail.

'Have you found Dr McKee?' Ms Ling asked.

'We have,' Janine said, 'he was involved in a road accident, he's fine, just cuts and bruises, but that's why he can't be here today. Now, we'll be talking to you each in turn, using the consulting rooms for privacy. Ms Ling, if you could come with us.'

Once Janine and Richard were settled with Ms Ling in the other room, the practice manager said, 'I've already made a list of Don's appointments yesterday, including his home visits.'

'Any of these names cause for concern?' Janine asked.

'No,' Ms Ling said.

'How was Dr Halliwell regarded?'

'Well respected, his list was always full, he was still a family doctor. You hear so much these days about people never seeing the same GP twice in a row, not knowing them but Don believed the doctor-patient relationship was essential. He would care for several generations of the same family. He was very popular.'

'Did anyone ever threaten him?'

'Oh, we all get our share of abuse,' Ms Ling said, 'it goes with the territory. But it's a small minority of people.'

'And what about formal complaints?' Richard said.

'Those too,' Ms Ling said.

'Anybody spring to mind? Anything current?' Janine said.

'Adele Young, her daughter Marcie.'

'Dr Halliwell attended Marcie's inquest on Monday?'

'That's right. Accidental death. Marcie was a heroin user. When she died, from an overdose of street drugs, Mrs Young instigated a formal complaint. She believed that Dr Halliwell had reduced Marcie's methadone dosage too quickly. The coroner fully exonerated Don. But the internal complaints process still has to run its course.'

'Sergeant Butchers will follow-up on these and any other complaints, if you can make sure he has all the notes. He's going to be based here for now,' Janine said, 'and will be going through Dr Halliwell's appointments.'

'Yes, of course,' Ms Ling said.

'How did Dr Halliwell get along with the rest of the staff?' Janine said.

'Fine,' Ms Ling said, 'well . . . except for Fraser.'

Janine felt her pulse speed up.

'They didn't always see eye to eye,' Ms Ling said, 'there was a confrontation yesterday.'

'A confrontation?' Richard said.

'Don informed Fraser that he wouldn't be made partner. Fraser didn't take it well.'

'Did he make any threats?' Richard said.

'No,' Ms Ling said, 'he was just very angry, disappointed.'

'Thank you,' Janine said. 'If you think of anything else do please tell Sergeant Butchers or contact any of us via the helpline.'

Ms Ling nodded.

As Janine went to ask Dr Gupta to come through, Ms Ling stopped to talk to someone at the fire door. Janine watched Ms Ling guide the caller, who was delivering an oxygen cylinder, along the corridor and heard him ask about Dr Halliwell. The murder had shaken the community to the core. Like Roper said, most of the gang violence was contained within the gangs and their associates but here was a middle class professional gunned down at his place of work. People needed reassurances, and they needed answers.

Receptionist Vicky Stonnall couldn't think of any reason why someone would harm Dr Halliwell. But when asked to describe the day in detail Vicky said, 'There were some sort of ructions going on, yesterday. Fraser had a face like thunder. You could have cut the air in chunks.'

'Do you know what it was about?' Janine said.

'Well, him and Dr Halliwell, they didn't really get on. Dr Halliwell, he's a bit old-fashioned. Was. It's weird,' she said, 'I keep having to remind myself he's dead. You never know, do you, you never know what's round the corner.'

'And the argument?' Janine said.

'Fraser's saying how he was relying on the partnership and how he's screwed now. Then he starts in about how Dr Halliwell runs his own little empire and no one else can have an opinion.'

'How did Dr Halliwell respond?' Richard said.

'Well . . .' Vicky grimaced, '. . .he didn't usually lose his temper but he went ballistic, he was under a lot of stress, he was shouting, really shouting at Fraser to get out, telling him he doesn't know what he's talking about.' She shuddered. 'It was horrible.'

* * *

'He was a good man, a good doctor, a friend,' Dr Gupta told Janine and Richard.

'All good?' Janine said.

'Well, we had to coax him a little with some of the new initiatives but he was highly regarded by his patients, his list was invariably full.'

'And his colleagues? Dr McKee?' Richard said.

There was a pause. Dr Gupta looked uneasy. 'Don didn't feel Fraser was right for us,' she said, 'in the long term. Fraser would complete his year, then he'd have to look elsewhere.'

'We understand there was a confrontation yesterday?' Janine said.

'That's right, a row, but you can't think that has anything to do with the shooting,' Dr Gupta said.

'We're not jumping to any conclusions,' Janine said, 'we're just gathering as much information as we can at the moment. Can you think of anything else, anything out of the ordinary, odd?'

'No,' she said, then she froze, her eyes cast upwards as though remembering.

'Dr Gupta?' Janine said.

'It may be nothing but—'

'Go on.' Janine said.

'On Monday, I saw a Range Rover outside, a black one, parked across the road. It was a little odd because surgery had already finished, so they weren't picking anyone up.' Janine thought of the 4x4 that had come after McKee. Could they be the same vehicle?

'Was there someone in it?' Richard said.

'A man. I couldn't see him properly, the windows were quite dark. And I didn't like to stare.'

'This was Monday?' Janine said.

'Yes,' Dr Gupta said, 'at six o'clock.'

'Did you see the car again?' Janine said.

'No.'

'Did you notice the registration?' Richard said.

'Sorry, no.'

'Thank you,' Janine said. 'Dr Gupta, we need someone to make a formal identification of the body and Mrs Halliwell has declined. Would you . . . ?'

'Of course,' she said.

'It will be sometime later today after the post-mortem,' Janine said. 'Thank you.'

* * *

Dawn Langan was so tearful, apparently in shock and they got next to nothing from her. In between crying, her eyes would cloud over, staring into the distance and Janine would have to repeat the question to get any reply.

'On Monday, do you remember seeing anyone parked across the street?' Janine said.

'No.'

'And did you notice anyone hanging around when you left on Tuesday?'

Dawn started to cry again. 'I'm sorry, it's just so awful.'

* * *

'Something Fraser McKee failed to mention,' Janine said as they walked to the car. 'A screaming row.'

'Shall we jog his memory?' Richard said.

'Definitely. It could be a motive but it's messy, isn't it? Halliwell sacks McKee in effect, McKee overreacts, some may say, and shoots Halliwell. Meanwhile, the Wilson gang are trashing McKee's house. McKee flees and is run off the road by forces unknown again maybe Wilson Crew affiliates — in a car similar to the one Dr Gupta saw the evening before.'

'Where's the gun?' Richard said.

'And why would McKee come to see us if he's the perpetrator?' Janine said.

Janine's phone rang. Shap calling. 'Boss, I'm at the garage. There's no match between the cars, they've found black paint on Halliwell's but nothing like that on McKee's. In fact, no sign that a second vehicle was involved in the crash at all. If he had been rammed, shunted off the road, they would expect to see scratches, paint samples and so on but there's nothing. *Nada.*'

'Interesting. Thanks Shap.' Janine relayed the news to Richard. 'Something else we need to speak to Fraser McKee about.' She checked her watch. 'I'm due at the post-mortem now — you go and sort out a duty solicitor for McKee and we'll question him under caution as soon as I'm back.'

CHAPTER 14

The ringing of the doorbell roused Norma from sleep. She was on her bed, fully clothed, a sour taste in her mouth and drool on the pillow.

Perhaps they'd leave, go away, if she just ignored it. But it went again, three short peals.

Norma wiped at her face, glimpsed herself in the mirror as she passed, face drawn, deep shadows under her eyes, hair tangled. No time to improve on her appearance.

Yvette was at the door. Had she not heard? Had the family not seen the news? The picture of Don, the headlines, *FAMILY GP SHOT DEAD*.

Yvette's family were from the Congo, recent immigrants. Sometimes Norma used a French word, Yvette's first language, to explain what she wanted from the teenager's playing.

'Mrs Halliday,' the girl smiled, her face bright, eyes clear. She didn't know. For a moment Norma considered letting her in, going ahead with a lesson anyway but swiftly realized this was foolish. She would not be able to listen to the music without getting upset. 'Yvette, I am sorry but the lesson is cancelled,' she said. 'My husband, he's . . . *il est mort. Je suis desolee.*'

The girl's smile disappeared and she swallowed. 'Oh, I am sorry,' she said and she scuffed one shoe against the step. Gawky.

'No more lessons,' Norma said, '*Finis*, finished.'

Yvette nodded. 'Yes,' she said, 'bye-bye. Thank you, *merci beaucoup*.' She walked away, down the drive.

'*Au revoir*,' Norma whispered. She had a sudden powerful memory of that wonderful summer in France, those weeks before she started university. Of Pierre, her first lover, her only lover apart from Don.

There was a small copse on the outskirts of the village, in a hollow below the road, where all the teenagers liked to meet. Pierre had arrived in the village over the winter, moving in with his grandmother, so Norma had not met him on previous holidays. He was the quiet type, on the edge of the group, enjoying the games and jokes, volunteering little. But his eyes were always on her and she felt the attraction too. He was sallow-skinned with brown eyes, long curling eyelashes and a crooked smile and he could play the harmonica.

The relationships in the group fluctuated. Some more serious than others, some of the local kids had a series of flings with les Anglais who visited and it was commonplace for couples to indulge in petting as the night wore on, moving away into the trees if things got more intense.

Norma kept a diary back then and each night chronicled the state of play with Pierre. On the second week, she moved away from the campfire with him, giddy from the wine but flushed with desire too. He had a rubber Johnny. She felt a lurch of embarrassment when he pulled it from his pocket and asked her to hold his lighter so he could see to put it on. But then he kissed her again and touched her and she didn't want it to stop.

She was level-headed enough to know it was only a holiday romance and when he asked for her address, so they could write, she had smiled and said she was moving to university so she didn't have one yet.

She never saw him again.

* * *

In the dining room, Norma got out her work diary. She made a list of current pupils and their phone numbers, seven in all not counting Yvette. Then she began to ring them. She rehearsed what she would say, a bereavement in the family, giving up teaching. In five cases she got an answerphone which made it easier. She spoke to a further three parents who sounded either shocked or embarrassed (they obviously knew about Don) and were as eager to keep things brief as she was. The other call, the last, was to Leo Johnson's house. Leo answered and said no, neither his mum nor dad were in. What did she want? Leo had an uncomfortable habit of saying whatever came into his head. Norma decided not to go into the reasons for terminating the lessons but just said, 'I'm not going to be doing lessons anymore, Leo, can you let your parents know?'

'Not on Saturday?'

'That's right. Not on Saturday. Not ever. I'm retiring.'

'You are quite old,' he said.

'I am, yes,' she said, 'bye-bye, Leo.'

'Bye, Miss. Miss?' he said quickly.

'Yes Leo?'

'Was that man your husband? The one what was shot?'

'Yes,' Norma said.

'Who shot him?'

'Nobody knows,' she said, 'the police are trying to find out.'

'OK Miss, bye Miss.'

Norma hung up the phone. She stared at the paper beside it where she had scrawled *dead*, *dead*, *dead* over and over and underlined it. 'Oh, Don,' she whispered.

She heard the door, and his footsteps and, shivering, she stumbled to the hall.

But there was no one there.

Just her.

Alone.

CHAPTER 15

'In good health, could have lived another forty years,' Susan, the pathologist, commented, 'clean liver and lungs, strong heart. Not always the way with doctors.'

Janine looked at the man on the table. He'd a strong face, large nose and highbrow. His clothes had been photographed, swept and taped for trace evidence then removed and sealed to be admitted into evidence. His body had been photographed and examined before being cleaned. The three wounds to his chest were vivid, shocking against the pallor of his skin but now overshadowed by the sweeping Y-shaped incision that the pathologist had made to carry out the internal exam.

Why, Janine thought? Why would anyone want to kill a GP? Someone who was providing a public service, someone who people trusted, relied on. Someone who tended to the sick, to babies and pensioners, the dying, those in pain. *First do no harm*. It seemed so peculiar.

If the man had been killed anywhere else she'd have been tempted to think of it as a case of mistaken identity but Halliwell had been locking up the surgery. Either whoever had shot him had done so deliberately, sought him out and killed him, or Halliwell had been an obstacle for someone who had come to the surgery carrying a handgun to some other end. Armed robberies these days usually focused on places with reasonable amounts of cash and minimal security: pubs, restaurants and the like. But the surgery didn't have any cash. They didn't store drugs in significant amounts. The last time the burglary happened they'd taken computers and prescription pads but they had done so cleverly, long gone before the police were alerted. No guns that time, no casualties.

'No defensive wounds,' Susan said, 'no sign of a scuffle, no skin under the nails.'

'The beauty of a gun,' Janine said, 'no contact needed between parties, means there's little or no exchange of trace material.'

'Harder for you,' Susan said.

'I'm hoping ballistics can give us a steer,' Janine replied.

'Any motive?' Susan asked, beginning to stitch the incision closed.

'Not sure,' Janine said. 'We've someone we're talking to, parted from the doctor on bad terms, shall we say.'

'Good luck,' Susan said.

'Thanks.' Janine replied, 'I've a feeling I'm going to need it.'

* * *

It was clear from the formality of the opening procedures and from Janine's tone that Fraser McKee was no longer simply being regarded as an innocent witness. Janine wasn't clear yet whether he had committed any crime but he had lied to the police, by omission, and that was a serious matter in the light of a murder.

'I'm concerned that you've been keeping information from us,' she said.

'I don't know what you mean,' Fraser McKee said.

'What can you tell me about the shooting of your colleague, Donald Halliwell?'

'Nothing,' McKee said. He looked at the solicitor by his side then back to Janine, though she noticed his eyes slid over hers.

'You're hiding something. Something about the shooting?' Janine said.

'No!' McKee looked terrified. 'Nothing. I've nothing to do with that. Honestly.'

"Really? On Tuesday afternoon you and Don Halliwell argued about your future at the practice,' she began. 'A couple of hours later he was dead.'

'That has nothing to do with me,' he said.

'Prove it,' Janine said, 'stop lying to us. The row with Don Halliwell?'

He looked up at the ceiling, took a deep breath. 'OK,' he said, 'I wanted to talk about being made a partner, I needed a rise. Don said they were going to let me go, that I wasn't right for them. I wasn't right!' He said derisively.

'Why was that?' Janine said.

'He couldn't stand the competition, that's what it was. I could see he was making mistakes and I let him know about it,' McKee said, an edge of malice in his tone. 'He didn't like that. Dissent in the ranks.'

'What mistakes?' Janine said.

'Marcie Young for one.'

'Dr Halliwell was fully exonerated at the inquest.'

'Not everyone thinks that was the right verdict,' McKee said.

'Including you?' Richard said.

'That's right.' McKee raised his chin.

'So yesterday you argued about your future at the practice, you claim that you left and went home. There you find that someone has done over your house and you flee in your car, you crash and then you come to us for help. What's all that about?' Janine said.

McKee hesitated, pale lashes blinking.

'This is a murder inquiry,' Janine reminded him. 'You've been less than honest with us. Now's the time to start.'

McKee said nothing, the muscles round his jaw jumped and flickered.

'Or perhaps,' Janine said, 'you actually returned to the surgery and waited for Dr Halliwell, furious that he was blocking your promotion, taking your job.'

'No, I didn't, I swear.'

'Tell me,' Janine said.

He pressed his lips together still reluctant.

'Traffic investigators have not found any evidence of another vehicle involved in your car crash,' Richard said.

'Omissions, inconsistencies,' Janine said, We could just send you on your way, you've not been honest with us so why should we believe you when you claim you're at risk of harm?'

Fear darted through his eyes. 'You can't do that,' he said.

'Try me,' Janine answered. 'You start talking, you stop wasting our time.'

McKee's shoulders dropped and he slumped back in his chair. 'I'm in debt, serious debt. I owe thousands. I got into a mess: student loan, credit cards, bought the house at just the wrong time. So,' he drew a breath, 'I went to this loans office, Barry Stroud, you know him? Sold him my debts but I couldn't keep up the instalments, it was crippling.' He stopped, closed his eyes.

'What then?' Richard said.

'Stroud offered me a way out, payment in kind. If I helped some friends of his break in to the surgery.'

'Yesterday?' Richard said.

'No, the time before,' said McKee, 'I had to make sure the alarm was off.'

'The alarm rang,' Richard said.

'Yeah, they set it off as they were leaving, to throw people off the track, so they wouldn't know they'd had inside help. These friends of Stroud's,' he curled a lip, 'I didn't know they were bloody gangsters.'

'Yesterday?' Janine said.

'They'd been on about organising a repeat performance, all relayed through Stroud. I never met them. But I couldn't

do it. Stroud kept threatening me. I said no. Then yesterday
. . . I got home and saw the house . . . I knew it'd be me next.
I didn't know where to go. I got in the car. Don's death was
on the news.' His voice shook, 'I panicked, I lost control of
the car. It was stupid.'

'The crash was an accident?' Richard said.

'Yes,' McKee said.

'And the black 4x4?' Richard said.

McKee shook his head. 'Doesn't exist.'

Janine was sick of his lies and half-truths, the way he
had confused the lines of inquiry and wasted their time and
resources.

'So no one ran you off the road?' she said.

'No — but they killed Don,' McKee's voice broke.

'Why would they do that?' Janine said.

He threw his arms out. 'As a warning. I wouldn't agree
to help them with the burglary so they killed him.'

'Bit extreme,' Richard said.

'Or in mistake for me, then,' McKee argued. 'Look, if
they find out . . .' He was still pale but beads of sweat had
broken out on his forehead. 'Can you . . . please, what sort
of protection do I get?'

'We want all this in a written statement,' Janine said, failing
to keep the irritation out of her voice. 'I advise you not to return
home and we can refer you to our witness support scheme.'

'But if I make a statement, if they know, they'll come
after me . . .'

'That's the point of the witness protection scheme,'
Janine said. 'You act as a witness for us and we protect you.'

McKee moved to stand up and Janine said, 'There's just
the matter of the charge.'

'Charge?' he stammered.

Janine nodded to Richard who said, 'Fraser McKee, I am
charging you with conspiracy to commit theft. You do not
have to say anything. But it may harm your defence if you
do not mention something which you later rely on in court.
Anything you do say may be given in evidence.'

McKee sat there, open-mouthed, aghast. What did he expect, Janine thought? A pat on the back? A free pass? Not going to happen. Even if the case came to court and the prosecution decided to grant him immunity he would still be expected to testify and witness protection was no joyride. He could kiss goodbye to his work as a doctor, he'd rarely see friends or family again. What a waste.

CHAPTER 16

The boards in the incident room had been updated to reflect what they now knew: McKee's involvement in the previous burglary, his financial problems, the Wilson Crew flagged up as behind the attack on his house. On the left, in the surgery section, there was a note about Dr Gupta's sighting of a black Range Rover and this was linked to the attack on Halliwell's car. Beneath a list headed 'grudges' were several names, including Adele Young, furnished by Butchers. The post-mortem results had been added.

'There is no connection between our murder case and the McKee incidents,' Janine said, 'separate inquiries. The investigation into the previous burglary we've passed over to serious crime. McKee's given his statement, he's out on bail and under the care of witness protection.

'The GMC?' Richard said.

'Notified,' Janine said.

'They'll have to strike him off,' Richard said.

'All that training,' Janine said, 'down the drain. Now, the post-mortem holds no surprises: our victim is in good health. There was nothing recovered that could lead us to the identity of the assailant or assailants. And I've had word through that the formal identification was made by Dr Gupta. So, looking afresh, what do we think? Is a botched robbery still the most likely scenario?'

'It doesn't explain the attack on Halliwell's car several hours earlier,' said Shap.

There were murmurs of agreement. 'For that,' Shap went on, 'we're looking for a black vehicle with a powerful engine, and the Range Rover seen by Dr Gupta on the Monday evening fits the specs.'

'If it's not an attempted burglary then what?' Janine said.

'Gang members, novices or younger brothers upping the stakes to make an impression, it's a cold-blooded hit and Halliwell's a random choice,' said Richard.

'He was in the wrong place at the wrong time?' Janine said. 'I still find it hard to see Halliwell as a gang target. The surgery's off the beaten track, if they were out to shoot someone why go there to do it?'

No one came up with any answers on that so Janine said, 'Other angles?'

'Can we rule out the family?' Richard said.

'There's no kids, just the wife,' Lisa said.

'Anything to suggest her involvement?' Janine said. 'Lisa, Shap, you broke the news?'

'She seemed genuinely upset.' Lisa said, 'She thought we were there about the damage to the car. She went into shock when she heard.'

'She could have been practising in front of the mirror,' Shap said.

'Shap,' Janine said, 'it's your faith in human nature gets me every time. OK, no concerns around the wife — but let's be thorough, Lisa check out that her earlier pupils did have their lessons as she said.'

Janine looked at the boards. 'Butchers, what have we got on patients so far?'

Butchers held up a DVD. 'Marcie Young's inquest. Janine nodded for him to play it and the team looked to the large screen up to the left of the incident boards. Butchers played the section where Adele Young gave her reaction to the reporters outside the court. 'Nothing will bring Marcie back but that doesn't mean I do nothing. It doesn't stop here,' she said firmly. She looked to be mixed race like her daughter, Janine thought. A black man behind her, a family member presumably — Marcie's father, Janine wondered — pushed forward. 'This isn't justice, this is a mockery.' He stabbed his fingers in the air. But Adele Young stopped him, 'Wait!' She turned back to the press. 'We'll get an independent review for Marcie and if that doesn't work we'll go to the ombudsman. These professionals need to start listening to us, to the families. And we need to stand up for ourselves and for the ones that are vulnerable, like Marcie, because no-one listens to them.'

'Good speech,' Janine said.

'She's got an axe to grind,' Richard said.

'Yeah, but she's going through the official channels. It'll be a fair few years before she's exhausted all the options. At that stage, maybe she'll think about taking it into her own hands.'

'Now someone's beaten her to it,' Shap said, 'maybe someone else who thought the official route was a waste of time.'

'Another disgruntled patient? Could be,' Janine said. 'Butchers you're talking to everyone who had an appointment with Halliwell on Tuesday. Use Shap if you need extra legs. And keep your ears open at the surgery.'

CHAPTER 17

The methadone replacement programme had a mixed press, Adele knew that. Some people hailed it as a proven route to breaking addiction, others pointed to a number of pitfalls, the addicts who sold the methadone to buy heroin, the problem of withdrawal from the methadone itself.

It was a chance, Adele thought, and Marcie responded better than she had imagined. It was still difficult to accept her daughter was taking the drug. Marcie usually did so in private in her bedroom, the dosage carefully set to give her just enough relief from the craving for heroin. Methadone mimicked the effects too, the rush, the slump of energy, nodding off. It was important to support her in altering her lifestyle and routine, to avoid other drug users, stay clear of the lifestyle, the locations of that world, the GP had explained.

Adele did all she could to encourage her. It would have helped if Marcie had been allowed back to school but she'd been excluded, no one wanted a junkie in the classroom. Or if she could have worked, that would've helped with her confidence but at almost fifteen she could only do a few hours and people in the area knew she was a user. She would not be trusted, not even to wash pots, until she had proved herself.

Maybe she'd go to college then, Adele thought. Find her feet, learn a trade, have a brighter future.

He's cut my dose,' Marcie had said slamming her bag onto the kitchen counter.

'Already?'

'Cut it in half.' There was confusion in her eyes and panic too.

Adele felt an answering burst of alarm. 'Why? Did he say why?'

'Just said it's the best thing, so I don't get too dependent.'

Of course you're dependent, Adele thought, you're an addict, this is a substitute. 'I'll have a word with him,' Adele said, 'we'll go in tomorrow. Tell them it's too soon. Yes?'

Marcie nodded.

* * *

Adele had to argue with the receptionist to get in to see him but she held her ground, just kept repeating that there was a serious problem with Marcie's medication that she needed to discuss with Dr Halliwell. It sounded silly after the third repetition but she kept her voice level and maintained eye contact, with Marcie fidgeting at her side, and as the queue built up behind her she felt the pressure increase on the woman, who finally said, 'Well, I can't give you a time, he's fully booked all morning.'

'Whenever,' Adele said. 'We need to see the doctor and we need to see him today.'

They waited an hour and twenty-five minutes before an apparent no-show meant they got called in.

He greeted them by name. He had a grandfatherly style, smiling, at least to start with.

'We feel the reduction in Marcie's dosage is too much, too soon,' Adele said.

The smile disappeared.

'I can assure you,' he said, 'that I'm satisfied she has stabilized on the current dose and best practice is now to reduce the amount.'

'But she's not—'

He held up a finger to silence her, his eyes now flat and cold. 'We do not simply want to replace one addiction with another.'

'It's not enough,' Marcie said, shakily.

His eyes flicked her way and back. 'I'll be the best judge of that,' he said. 'In my opinion your best chance of recovery from drug abuse rests in sticking with my treatment plan. Otherwise we are all wasting our time.'

Adele felt a flush of anger, the afterburn of resentment. 'Based on what?' she said, sounding more bullish than she meant to.

'Based on a lifetime's experience in medical practice.'

'We could get a second opinion,' Adele said.

'That is your prerogative. The relationship between doctor and patient is one of trust and cooperation. If that breaks down . . .'

He was threatening them, the arrogant wanker. Adele had no idea how easy or hard it might be to find a new GP, to get the help Marcie needed. And if it took some time, if there was a gap in her treatment, she could soon be back on the streets.

'A cut in half is a big step,' Adele said, 'and patients must vary. If that was staggered, say over a month or two.' She spoke too quickly, babbling.

Dr Halliwell watched her with unforgiving eyes and then said, 'If I thought that was appropriate then that's what I would have done. We can't all be experts.'

Marcie made a little sound, a sigh or a laugh, Adele couldn't tell.

'She's my daughter,' Adele said, 'and I believe her when she says it's too early, that she won't be able to cope.'

'She's my patient, Mrs Young. Addicts will do anything to get a fix, perhaps Marcie is not as committed to recovery as she should be.'

'How dare you!' Adele said. 'Why won't you listen to what she's saying instead of slagging her off? She needs your help!' She was trembling with rage, her face hot, her ears singing.

'I'll thank you to lower your voice,' he said sharply, 'or leave.' He turned to Marcie. 'I'll see you next week. Believing you can do it is half the battle. This may well be a bout of cold feet.' He sat back and gestured to the door, his face set.

Adele clamped down on the anger, she needed to in order to deal with Marcie. All that mattered was that Marcie didn't just give up and stop trying.

'You are going to do this,' Adele said on the way home, 'and I'll help.'

'How?' the girl said.

'Any way I can. It'll be all right,' she said, trying to sound truthful. 'It might not be easy but I know you can do it. It'll be all right.' She tried to smile then turned away so Marcie would not see the worry.

The words were a prayer. And a lie.

* * *

Adele knew, from her own smoking habit, that addiction acted upon the brain as much as the body, that the whisper of voices in your head was as much responsible for relapse as the physical cravings. The times Adele had tried to stop smoking she had to erect barriers in her mind to prevent those thoughts from entering at all; because it was only five minutes from *just one won't hurt* or *you can't keep this up* or *you deserve a smoke, today, don't you?* to that guilt-ridden sprint to the corner shop and twenty Lambert & Butler. So she could sense that Marcie's belief that her new dosage was inadequate could, oh so easily, translate into her 'just needing a proper fix'.

They were watching Big Brother but Marcie was distracted, getting up and down for crisps, then a biscuit, then Bombay mix; shifting on the sofa, making the leather squeak, rubbing at her leg then her stomach, as if her skin was crawling: one of the responses to withdrawal Adele had read about in the leaflets and online.

'It might take a day or two to get used to it,' Adele said. 'Your body would have to adjust, give it a couple of days and you'll feel much better.'

Marcie shot her a look, sullen. She bit her nails. Adele stopped herself commenting. *Christ, if that helps then go for it.*

When Howard came home, she cooked chicken fillets, oven chips and peas hoping the food might fill some of the hunger that Marcie was feeling. Adele watched Marcie eat, waiting until she went upstairs to tell Howard about their visit to the doctor.

'She'll be all right.' He reached over and rubbed Adele's shoulder. 'It's bound to get easier.'

'Just don't leave any money about.'

He turned to look at her, muting the sound on the TV. *You really think?* his expression said.

Adele shrugged. 'Just don't.' She lay away most of the night, listening for the creak of the top step or the click of the front door but Marcie never left her room.

Adele was on early the following day, six till two, serving food at the airport. Work was purgatory. She resisted the temptation to ring Marcie every five minutes. Howard was there until mid-day and that meant Marcie would only have two and a half hours on her own, as long as Adele's bus was on time.

When Adele got home, Marcie was safe on the sofa. Adele felt as though she'd been holding her breath all day long. 'Do you want a brew?' Adele asked Marcie, who nodded. She looked miserable, preoccupied.

'Can I have a cig?' Marcie asked when Adele brought her drink.

'Of course.' She didn't hesitate. 'Here.' She passed the packet. 'In the yard.' Adele never smoked in the house, well, very, very rarely. Howard didn't like it and she didn't want the place smelling like an ashtray.

It was cool outside, a sharp wind. Marcie hunched her shoulders up, and smoked like an old hand. Adele shivered, the smoke and her breath both coming in great clouds. 'How're we doing?' she said.

Marcie creased her nose, then tears filled her eyes.

'Hey,' Adele said gently, 'it will get better. And I am so proud of you, you know that, don't you?'

Marcie gulped. 'What? Your junkie daughter?'

'My girl,' Adele said, 'and you're trying, it must be so hard and you're sticking with it and that is totally brilliant.' She hurried the last words, sensing her voice might break and not wanting to upset Marcie and show that sort of emotion.

They got a take-away from the Bengal for tea. Adele found it hard to eat, to force food down her gullet. The knots in her stomach got worse. She smoked more than usual and by bedtime she had a thumping headache over one eye.

Another early shift tomorrow. She did sleep but fitfully and the alarm woke her at five.

She opened her eyes. Her phone was gone. A kick in her belly. A fleeting moment's thought told her that she *had* brought it upstairs last night. She felt under the pillow. Her purse was still there. She got up and went straight to Marcie's room knowing already that it was too late, that the room would be empty, that Marcie had gone.

The next time Adele saw her she was laid out on a mortuary table, covered in a sheet.

CHAPTER 18

Wednesday was Pete's night for the kids, though it tended to be Tom who spent most time with him: Pete would put Charlotte to bed and Eleanor was of an age where time on her own in her bedroom was preferable to any interaction with either of her boring parents. When Janine pulled into the drive she was surprised to see there was no sign of Pete's car outside the house.

Janine went in and called out 'Hello? Tom?'

She found him in the living room, sprawled on the couch, a game on the TV.

'Where's your Dad?' Janine said.

Tom shrugged, never taking his eyes from the screen.

'Oh, he's probably got held up with Alfie,' Janine said, annoyed that she had to make up excuses for Pete. 'Did you ring him?'

Tom gave a shake of his head.

Janine heard Eleanor coming downstairs and went into the hallway to catch her.

'Your dad's not been, then?' Janine said.

'Who?' Eleanor said, not breaking her stride.

Janine pulled out her phone and dialled Pete's landline. His voice mail was on. 'Hi, you've reached Pete, Tina and

Alfie. Leave a message.' *All very cosy but what about your other kids?*

'Pete,' Janine said after the beep, 'Tom was expecting you tonight. Can you call me back? Be nice if you called him too, or text, smoke signals, whatever.'

It's not fair, Janine thought, she hated the idea of Tom waiting for his dad, of his anticipation turning to disappointment. Pete had sworn that he'd have regular time with them, even if it had to be less time than before with Alfie's arrival. She was sick of having to nag and cajole and negotiate with Pete. Why couldn't he just get his act together and do as he promised?

Janine took a breath and then went upstairs to check on Charlotte. She was in bed and fast asleep.

Eleanor came back up and Janine went onto the landing. 'Did you put Charlotte to bed?'

'Someone had to,' she said, heading for her room.

'Thanks,' Janine said.

'Add it to what you owe me for last night,' Eleanor said over her shoulder.

Brilliant! Now Eleanor would be charging her for everything. Perhaps if Pete had to chip in too, that'd concentrate his mind.

CHAPTER 19

Day Three — Thursday

The break came on Thursday morning. The team were collating statements and reports, cross-referencing information
from the inquiry when Lisa answered a call to the incident
room. 'Boss, ballistics.'

Janine took the phone from Lisa. 'Good morning, DCI
Lewis speaking.'

'Morning. We've a result on the bullets in the Donald
Halliwell case. The same weapon was used in a non-fatal
shooting here two years ago. The perpetrator was one Aaron
Matthews. Matthews was convicted but the gun was never
found.'

Janine felt the fizz of adrenalin in her veins. 'Thank you,'
she said, 'excellent news.' She ended the call aware of the
expectant faces around her. 'We've a match,' she said. 'Aaron
Matthews.' Janine waved at Shap to get on the computer and
look up the details. There was a buzz of anticipation in the
room, a quickening of the energy. It was just what they needed
after being jerked about by Fraser McKee. A solid lead.

Shap logged on to the database, murmuring, 'Press red
on your remote now.' He clicked on the criminal record of

Aaron Matthews. A photograph appeared of a young black man, along with his charge sheet and related intelligence. 'Known associate of the Wilson Crew,' Shap read out loud, 'twenty months inside for assault with a firearm. Released last month. The timing's sweet.'

'Butchers, establish where he's living, now,' Janine said, 'Lisa — warrants, Richard — run the name past DCS Roper, make sure Matthews is not one of their inner circle, don't want to tread on their toes.'

'He could still be carrying,' Shap said.

'We'll pull in an armed response unit,' Janine said. 'All other lines of inquiry parked while we follow up on Matthews.' She relished the feeling of excitement, the prospect that real progress was in sight, and with it the chance of catching the murderer and answering the question that plagued her most. Why?

* * *

The area around Aaron Matthews' maisonette flat had been secured, traffic turned away, residents and passers-by prevented from entering. Janine noticed a bystander at the far end of the street busy with a camera phone. The armed response team with their specialist training would approach the flat and hopefully detain the suspect. Janine, Richard, Shap and Lisa waited on the pavement below, out of harm's way. The block was two storeys high and Matthews' flat was on the top storey, a blue painted door in the middle of the row.

Janine watched. Her stomach clenched in anticipation, as the leader of the armed unit signalled to his crew to move in. They climbed the stairs at the side of the building swiftly and funnelled along the walkway. The armed officers stopped and took up formation either side of the door. The leader signalled to his unit again then hammered hard on the door, speaking loudly enough for those in the street below to hear. 'This is Greater Manchester Police. Open the door. Open the door. Police.'

There was a moment's pause, Janine's mouth felt dry, then the blue door opened. Aaron Matthews was visible. 'What's going on?' he demanded.

'Arms on your head,' the leader said.

Matthews complied.

The officer used a metal detector wand and swept it down in front of Matthews, searching for a gun.

'Turn around,' the officer said. Matthews shuffled round and the officer moved the wand over his back and down to his feet. 'Clear,' he announced.

'Step onto the landing.'

Matthews stepped outside.

'Hands behind your back.'

Matthews was escorted down the steps to Janine. She nodded to Lisa to cuff the suspect and make the formal caution on arrest.

* * *

Lisa snapped the cuffs on Matthews and began, 'Aaron Matthews, I am arresting you on suspicion of murder. You do not have to say anything. But it may harm your defence—'

Sudden movement and Matthews bolted. Lisa went after him, shouting to him to stop, Shap just behind her. The uniformed officers who were securing the scene gave chase too.

Aaron dodged through the alley that led to the precinct. Lisa forced herself to run faster, her heart thumping, her legs burning with the effort. Matthews jumped over bollards leading to a parking area and Lisa followed, gaining on him. As he turned again, he skidded and slipped, giving her a chance to close the distance between them. She willed herself on, ignoring the cramp biting in her calf and the sharp pain in her windpipe. Closer still, she lunged and grabbed his shoulder, spun him round. Forced him to stop.

Panting, and ignoring all the people gawking on the sidelines, Lisa walked Matthews back to the cars. Janine nodded and Lisa felt a ripple of relief. Thank God she had caught him. She should have considered that he'd be a flight risk. She should have got him into the car sooner.

Now, trying to hide the way she was shaking, she put him in the back of the car and got into the passenger seat. One of the uniformed officers was driving them back.

'Got something to hide?' Lisa said.

'I freaked right, you talking about murder. What murder?' Matthews was agitated, eyes livid.

'Come on, Aaron,' Lisa said, 'Dr Donald Halliwell.'

'No way!' he protested.

'We've got some very good evidence says otherwise,' Lisa said.

'You can't have, I had nothing to do with it. Nothing. I'm not a part of all that anymore.'

'Really? Same gun,' Lisa said.

'I sold that,' Matthews said, 'I walked away — from all of it.'

'Yeah, right,' Lisa said.

'You think it's easy? There's places I can't go, people — I have to steer well clear. And now you lot come and fuck it all up. If they hear about this, they'll think I'm a snitch, you might as well put a target on my back.' He turned his face away and looked out of the side window. Lisa's heart was still loud in her ears, head spinning from the rush. She sat back and relaxed her shoulders, looking forward to seeing what happened once the boss got Aaron Matthews in an interview room.

CHAPTER 20

Butchers had finalised the timeline for Dr Halliwell's day on Tuesday, his appointments at morning and evening surgery and the home visits in-between and had now turned his attention to collating information on patients who had made complaints.

There was a knock at the door and Vicky Stonnall popped her head in. 'Coffee?'

'Yeah, thanks. Doctor Halliwell and Doctor Gupta were both quite settled here?'

'It's a cushy number,' Vicky said. 'He was nudging a hundred thousand, and Doctor Gupta's husband's a consultant so they're steaming rich.'

'Big money,' Butchers said.

'It's the business to be in, that or city trading. And they don't even have to do out-of-hours, anymore. Not like your lot,' Vicky said.

'I make a decent enough living,' Butchers said. There was only him to spend the money.

'Yeah, but it's all broken marriages and living for the job, isn't it, your line? I wouldn't fancy it,' Vicky said.

'Wouldn't you?' Butchers said, deciding not to dwell on his own trail of dead relationships.

'You fraternising with me?' Vicky said, her mouth in a little smirk.

'Fraternising?' Butchers said. 'You're not the enemy are you?'

'Not last time I looked. Coffee, then.' She disappeared.

Butchers leant forward and pressed the tannoy button. 'Three sugars please.' The sound echoed from the waiting room, making him smile.

After a few minutes he got up and went through to reception. Vicky was coming downstairs from the staff lounge and kitchen, with a tray of coffee. She handed Butchers his and offered him a plate of biscuits. Butchers chose two. 'Ta.'

Vicky took her own coffee round the counter and sat in her chair.

Butchers leant against the counter. She was alright Vicky, he reckoned, down to earth, approachable.

'If someone was a bit dizzy, like,' Butchers said, 'what would that be?' He'd been surrounded by posters exhorting people to adopt a healthy lifestyle, lose weight, take exercise. It was getting to him.

Dawn Langan came out of the nurse's room and Butchers nodded in greeting. She still looked very shaken, peaky, her blonde hair greasy.

'Coffee, Dawn?' Vicky said.

'No, thanks,' Dawn edged behind reception and began sorting through a box of glassine envelopes with stickers and vials in. For blood samples were they?

'It could be loads of things, dizziness,' Vicky answered Butchers. 'Could be your blood pressure. Do you get it checked? Dawn'll do it for you.'

Dawn glared at Vicky and Butchers said, 'No, it's OK.' He bit into a biscuit. 'Seems there's been a fair few complaints about Dr Halliwell,' he said.

'Well, he's been here a long time,' Vicky said, 'they all get some.'

'What did you think of him?' Butchers said.

'He was all right,' she said. Butchers waited, he'd heard a 'but' in there. 'Well,' Vicky went on, 'he liked being the boss. Didn't want his patients chipping in with ideas. Doctor knows best, that sort of thing.'

'And mistakes?' Butchers said.

'He never made mistakes — isn't that what they used to teach 'em? Doctor is never wrong.'

Dawn Langan straightened up, spots of colour high on her cheeks and turned on Vicky Stonnall. 'He was a good man. How can you stand there and talk about him like that? You make me sick.' She swung past Vicky, marched to the nurse's room and slammed the door.

'She wants to watch her blood pressure,' Butchers said. 'Is she usually so touchy?'

'She's upset,' Vicky said.

'It's not just me, then?' Butchers said. 'Every time I appear, she vanishes.'

'It's nothing personal, it's the situation, isn't it?' Vicky said.

'Don't shoot the messenger,' Butchers said.

'Not the best choice of words, that.' Vicky grinned.

Butchers finished his coffee and returned to his task. He'd heard that they were arresting Aaron Matthews and thought about it. Matthews had previous form, hadn't been out of prison long. So what then — he'd tried to break in, thinking he could nick some blank prescriptions to flog, some second-hand computers but ran into Halliwell who was locking up. Or did he know Halliwell? Was there some history there?

Telling himself it was a long shot, Butchers scanned the patient list, and there he was. Had to be the same lad. Aaron Matthews. Butchers stretched, grunted with satisfaction and picked up the phone.

CHAPTER 21

Janine ordered a gunshot residue test — though it was over thirty six hours since the shooting and anyone with half a brain who had used a firearm would know to change their clothes and wash well to remove the evidence. But she'd seen enough incompetent killers to hope they still had some chance.

She tried to ring Pete from her office while Aaron Matthews was consulting with the duty solicitor, annoyed that Pete had not even returned her call or made any attempt to apologize for not showing up last night.

'Can't talk now,' Pete said quickly, when she got through,' I'll call you back.' And he hung up before she had chance to say a word. She bit down on her resentment and went to see whether Matthews was ready yet but was met by Richard coming into the incident room, waving a piece of paper.

'Prepared statement,' Richard said.

Everyone groaned. Janine felt a twitch of irritation. Issuing a prepared statement was a clear indication that Aaron Matthews would refuse to answer any questions put to him.

Richard read from the statement, 'I have no knowledge about the offence or those involved. I am not involved in any criminal activity and am not associating with any known criminals.'

'We'll still give it a go,' Janine said. 'Richard? Lisa?'

Lisa grinned. She was on a roll, Janine thought, first making the arrest and now a role in the interview.

'Your notes are complete,' Richard said to Lisa, referring to her documentation of the arrest. Lisa nodded, and passed them to him. He scanned them and signalled to Janine that they were ready.

'Off you go, then,' Janine said, trying to sound brighter than she felt. If Aaron Matthews was 'no comment' then all they had were the ballistics linking Matthews to the weapon and on its own that wasn't enough to prove he was the perpetrator. She watched Richard and Lisa go.

The phone rang and Shap answered. 'Butchers for you, boss,' Shap said.

Janine took the phone, 'Butchers?'

'Aaron Matthews, he's a patient of Dr Halliwell's.'

'Is he now?' Janine said, 'Thanks, I'll let Richard know, he's about to go in to interview. A prior relationship could give us motive.'

* * *

Lisa was nervous, she'd not done many suspect interviews yet but she was grateful that the boss had given her the opportunity: she could just as easily have put Shap in with DI Mayne.

Lisa had gone through the formalities for the recording: who was in the room, the date and time, and then DI Mayne said to Matthews, 'Where were you between the hours of six and seven pm on Tuesday evening?'

'No comment.'

'The weapon used in this shooting is the one that was in your possession, the one you used in the commission of your last offence. Where is that gun now?'

'No comment.'

Aaron reminded Lisa of some of the lads she was at school with, bright enough and could have made something of themselves if they hadn't been drawn into the gangs, swayed by the peer pressure, the lure of easy money, the sense of belonging and of protection that a gang offered. Not much use when you got caught, though. Aaron had already done time. Had he learnt nothing? Was this it — the pattern for the rest of his life?

'Shortly after your arrest today,' DI Mayne said, 'you claimed that you had sold that weapon.'

'Inspector,' the duty solicitor interrupted, a fake smile on her lips, 'my client was not under caution then, according to PACE rules.'

What? Lisa felt the bottom drop out of her stomach.

The DI looked stunned.

'Police and Criminal Evidence—' the duty solicitor began.

'I know what it stands for,' Richard cut her off.

Lisa felt physically sick. She had cautioned Matthews, hadn't she? She'd begun it, she was certain of that and then . . .Oh God . . . He'd legged it and she hadn't had chance to finish it. And when she caught him and got him in the car she'd been so pumped on adrenaline she hadn't even thought about it. She'd written in her notes that she'd issued the caution on arrest without even thinking about it. Shit!

'Interview suspended,' DI Mayne said.

Lisa followed him to his office. Her stomach churned and her pulse raced.

The DI was furious, his eyes hard and an expression of disgust on his face as he held up her notes. 'It's here in black and white,' he said.

'I started it but then he did his great escape and I forgot to complete it,' she said.

'And forgot to tell me? Christ, Lisa, he's our chief suspect, he's a gang-banger who we can link to the gun and we can't use a bloody word of it. Nothing that he said in that car. And now he's no comment.'

'I'm really sorry,' she said.

'Go,' he said, 'just go. We'll discuss what this means for your prospects tomorrow.'

Lisa hid in the Ladies for a while, wanting to cry and kicking herself, wanting to run away, to go home but she had to face them, all of them, knowing that she'd screwed up.

She was making her way back to the incident room when Shap stopped her.

'Hey, Mother Theresa,' he said under his breath, 'why'd you go and hold your hands up? It's your word against his. You should have just fronted it out. Ten years back no-one would have given a toss. Who are they going to believe? That toerag or a serving police officer?'

Lisa shook her head. She couldn't be like Shap. Didn't want to be.

* * *

There was an awkward edge to the atmosphere as Lisa arrived back in the incident room.

The boss, DI Mayne at her side, gave Lisa a look; not angry more let down, like she'd expected better from Lisa and Lisa felt wretched.

'His gunshot residue's clear,' the boss said, 'that was a stretch, anyway, given the time lapse. It doesn't mean he didn't fire the gun. He could have cleaned up.'

'It weakens any case against him,' DI Mayne said.

'He used the same weapon before,' Shap said, 'he resisted arrest, he won't talk to us. He's way ahead of anyone else as a candidate. All this crap about turning over a new leaf is just that — crap.'

'He might be telling the truth,' the boss said.

'Pigs . . . sky,' Shap said, 'Matthews is good for it. He and Halliwell knew each other.'

'There's nothing from his flat. Nothing that places him at the scene,' DCI Lewis said.

DI Mayne sighed, he looked like he wanted to kick something.

'It's a setback but that's all it is. We keep working it,' the boss said, 'we bring him back when we've cause.'

'He's out on licence,' Shap said, 'we could do him for resisting arrest.'

'I want to do him for murder,' DI Mayne said sharply. 'Lisa, get rid of him.'

Of course it had to be her, she'd messed up and now she'd be the one to have her nose rubbed in it, releasing Matthews from custody, watching him walk.

* * *

'Do you want me to have a word with Lisa?' Janine said to Richard on her way out.

'She's gone already,' Richard said, 'but, I'll deal with it. I'm seeing her tomorrow.'

'She's a good copper, you know, she shows promise.'

Richard gave her a look.

'We all make mistakes,' Janine said.

'Yeah,' he said, 'and we have to accept the consequences.'

CHAPTER 22

Norma recognized the sense of dislocation, the numbness from before. She was eight months pregnant at the time. She'd been into town that morning round the department stores, buying the final few items on her list. The nursery was finished, pale green walls with white and yellow woodwork, curtains that she had made herself. The material had a white background with drawings of animals on, all sorts, like those in the ark.

She had considered NCT classes but Don was dubious. 'They're obsessed with natural childbirth,' he said, 'they'll spout ridiculous nonsense about intervention. You'd be better off going to the hospital classes.' So that was that.

She was putting the changing mat and the nappies away in the alcove cupboard in the nursery when she felt the cramp. Was this a Braxton Hicks? Norma had read plenty of books about pregnancy and labour. When she went to the toilet she found blood in her knickers. A show? First babies were usually late but perhaps this one was an exception. Should she wait to see if labour started? Her mind buzzed with indecision. She felt another cramp deep inside but there was no tightening across her abdomen, just the dragging feeling that came and went quite quickly. She rubbed her belly, tracing the baby. She knew the head was partially engaged, and the round bump she could feel at the top was most likely the baby's bottom. She wanted to ask Don what to do but had no way of contacting him apart from leaving a message with the office at the medical school and then hoping someone would actually pass it on.

There wasn't a lot of blood but it was more than just spotting. As for a 'show' she would have expected something more substantial as the plug in the cervix came away. She'd talk to the midwives before doing anything else.

When she rang the number she had, they advised her to come in. 'Just so we can check everything is OK.'

She called a taxi and didn't have any more discomfort so by the time she arrived she was pretty sure that she wasn't in labour and was starting to feel a little foolish.

The midwife listened to her account and asked a few questions before inviting Norma to get up on the examination couch, where she gently pressed her abdomen and then listened with a stethoscope. She asked Norma to wait where she was for a moment.

The moment stretched on into minutes and Norma stared at the ceiling and the fluorescent light. She wanted to wee. Perhaps it was a urinary infection?

The midwife returned with a doctor who also listened with a stethoscope and then asked Norma when she had last felt the baby move.

Last night? This morning? 'I'm not sure. I don't know,' she said, her voice high and wavering.

'I'm a little concerned,' the doctor said, 'we can't make out the baby's heartbeat so we're going to take you through to ultrasound and get a scan.'

She knew then it was too late. If there'd been any chance for the baby they would have rushed her into an OR for an emergency caesarean.

'My husband,' she said quietly to the midwife, 'please can you let him know I'm here? He's at the school of medicine. Don Halliwell. Fourth year.'

'I'll do that now.'

They wouldn't let her walk, she had to wait for a porter to bring a wheelchair and take her down for the sonograph. She pressed her hands over her belly, hoping she might detect some movement there, that the baby might suddenly wake and twist and kick and everything would be alright again.

* * *

The house felt like a tomb. Norma turned the heating up. As the radiators warmed, making knocks and gurgles in the pipes, the bones of the house creaked and clicked in response. But she was still cold.

She was used to her own company. Most of her days had been spent alone, the only interaction was with the pupils who came after school or on Saturdays for a half hour lesson. But she was never alone at night. Don was always there.

Always.

She knew that some of the GPs attended conferences, eager to follow new developments in medicine and no doubt enjoy the socializing and break from routine but Don had never gone.

And whatever affairs he had had were limited, she presumed, to evenings in hotel rooms returning to the marital bed by the early hours.

He had sworn to look after her and he had. Until now.

She sensed someone in the house. She went to each room in turn, searching under the beds and cupboards, behind the long curtains. She left the doors wide open and sat at the top of the stairs, hugging her knees, and listened.

She heard it then, Don's voice, quiet, 'Norma.' Her skin went to gooseflesh. 'Norma.' It was coming from downstairs.

With her heart hammering she went down, holding tight to the banister, in fear of falling.

She stood in the kitchen, her eye roaming over the high-gloss cabinets, the double sink, the Aga. She cocked her head, heard only the drone of the big fridge-freezer. It was too big.

The fridge, the house and everything in it. So large she was lost. There were only two of them for heaven's sake.

'Norma.' From the hall.

She went and stood at the bottom of the stairs. It began to rain outside, the wind hurled drops of rain hard against the window. Norma glanced at the portrait on the wall, a woman staring out from a woodland scene. Her look was hard, accusing.

'Norma.' She whirled round. She couldn't see him but he was here. She could smell him, sense him. He shouldn't still be here.

'Go away,' she said. 'Please, go away.'

The rain rattled on the glass, a gust of wind moaned through the keyhole in the door.

Norma took the painting down and left it, face against the wall.

She needed something to calm her down, quiet his voice. She'd go mad otherwise.

'Go away,' she said once more. What did he want with her? Why wouldn't he leave her be?

CHAPTER 23

Janine tried Pete before leaving for home and got the answer-phone message again.

He was avoiding her. Irritated, she felt her cheeks glow. He was acting like a teenager, missing his night with Tom and then ducking all attempts to face up to it.

If the mountain won't come to Muhammad. . .

Janine had never been inside the townhouse that Pete and Tina shared near Salford Quays. On occasions she had dropped the kids off there but it was far more usual for Pete to ferry them from her house.

It was dark and a wind was blowing leaves and litter about as Janine parked outside.

Twee, she thought looking at the house, ill-proportioned then she caught herself. Get a grip — don't be petty.

She used the door-knocker, three loud raps, and waited. She heard the baby crying and it grew louder until Pete opened the door, Alfie over one shoulder, legs pumping, head twisting, face red with exertion.

An expression of dismay crossed Pete's face.

'Tom was expecting you last night,' Janine said, 'we all were. I left you messages.' She spoke loudly to be heard above the squalling.

'Not now,' Pete said and she saw from the set of his lips and the light in his eyes that he was very angry.

'When then? You've been avoiding—'

He held up a hand to stop her. The baby bawled.

'Not now,' Pete said again.

'Pete, Tom needs you—'

He shut the door on her.

She stood there, dumbfounded.

She was tempted to bang on the door again, hammer on it until he had to respond but she judged it would not be a wise thing to do.

She simmered with outrage all the way home, holding imaginary conversations with him in her head. Re-running the doorstep encounter so that she got what she wanted: an honest apology and a renewed commitment to his duties as a father.

She chewed it over as she helped Tom with his homework and found his missing PE kit, as she left a note for the nanny with a request to get some fresh fruit and sliced bread for school lunches. She probed at it like poking at a sore tooth while she got changed and ready for bed.

She wouldn't let him off the hook, she decided, she would ring him every day until they sorted out what on earth he was playing at. Plonker.

When she slept she dreamt of going to the house and shooting Pete on the doorstep. It should have been satisfying, comic even, but it filled her with a dark dread as she desperately tried to stop the blood and revive him.

CHAPTER 24

That day, the day the police came to Adele's door, was a Tuesday, a bright, sunny Tuesday and she hadn't seen Marcie for four days. Her stomach fell and then there was a moment when she forced hope to rise in her chest. Marcie had been caught stealing, that would be it. Nothing they hadn't handled before. Nothing they—

'Dead,' the woman said once they were in the house. There were other words, *for identification, sorry, suspected overdose, post-mortem* but Adele barely heard them. Acid flooded her veins, stripping her nerves, burning her skin. She felt the ground beneath her buckle and crack. Howard was calling to her, holding her. She was hitting out, screaming, but the gestures, the cries came from a long way away through the dense, cold clouds of shock.

It was hard to remember the sequence of things, the memories were like a slideshow, a horror-show of images. At some point Dr Halliwell had come, bringing condolences and the offer of tranquilizers. 'To help you deal with these difficult few days.' Christ, talk about the art of understatement.

There had been the waiting till they could go to identify Marcie. Then they wouldn't let her touch her, wouldn't let her anywhere near. It was clinical, impersonal, she could've been looking through the glass to choose a piece of meat.

Adele tried to explain and said, 'Howard, I want to be with her.'

'You're welcome to sit here,' the attendant said, 'we could get you a chair.'

Adele looked back at her daughter, shook her head. 'That's not what I mean, I want to hold her.'

'Once the body's released—' the woman began.

'How long will that take?' Howard said.

'A few days,' she said, sounding uncertain.

Adele wanted to press through the glass, lift her daughter up, take her home, make her warm and clean, breathe life back into her, put cornrows in her hair and kiss her eyelids. She wanted a fucking fairy tale and it wasn't going to happen.

* * *

She worked it out one night, Marcie had been alive for fifteen years, four months, and two days. With her gone, the centre of Adele's world, the focus of her life went too. And her future. Adele would have drowned in her grief had it not been for a growing flame of anger at Marcie's death; the sense that it was not an inevitable outcome but one that Adele had feared and tried so hard to prevent.

CHAPTER 25

Lisa couldn't settle, replaying the events of the day over and over: racing after Matthews, triumphant when she caught him, the look on DI Mayne's face when he realised she had failed to follow procedure, feeling stupid, so stupid.

She pushed away the pasta she had made, too queasy to eat. Their prime suspect and she'd ruined their chance at questioning him. They knew Aaron Matthews had been part of the Wilson crew, and in his previous offence he had used the gun that later killed Halliwell. He was also a patient of Halliwell's. Had he a motive for shooting the GP? Or did Halliwell just get in the way? Lisa felt confused, muddled. Now they would have to start again, see if there was anything else to link Matthews to the crime.

Why wait for tomorrow, she asked herself? There was no way she was going to do anything staying home but sit here feeling sorry for herself and working up a panic about what DI Mayne would decide to do with her tomorrow. She might as well put the time to good use, see if she could find anything else.

She picked up her ID, turned off the lights and set off.

CHAPTER 26

Opening the morning team briefing, Janine started with the weapon. 'Back to basics. Our killer had access to a gun; Aaron Matthews' gun. Two possibilities.' Janine counted them off on her fingers. 'Matthews fired the gun; or our killer obtained the gun from Matthews at some juncture and used it. We couldn't hold Matthews but he is still our number one suspect.

'The Range Rover, the one that was seen outside the surgery on Monday and was used to ram Halliwell's car, I bet that's our killer's,' Shap said.

'Let's see if we can find a car like that on local CCTV approaching the surgery on the Tuesday prior to the shooting or on the Monday when Dr Gupta saw it. Lisa can you do that?'

'Yes, boss.'

'We've still not found the briefcase,' Janine said, 'are any of these people suddenly chucking prescriptions around?' She pointed to the boards, all the names connected to the inquiry. 'Is anyone bragging about a hit? Meanwhile we throw everything we can at links to Aaron Matthews: friends and family, the gang network, hangers-on, wannabees.'

'Boss,' Lisa raised her hand. 'I found a connection last night.'

'Go on,' Janine said.

'Aaron Matthews' uncle is Howard Urwin,' Lisa said, 'Adele Young's partner.'

Janine felt the hairs on her neck lift. The atmosphere in the room shifted. Richard turned to face Lisa, Shap sat up in his seat and Butchers leant forward.

'Has Urwin any criminal record?' Janine asked.

'No, boss,' Lisa said.

'Any association with the Wilson Crew?' Richard said.

'No, boss.'

'You found this out how?'

'Did some digging,' Lisa said. 'Urwin had given a character reference for Aaron Matthews when he was on trial, how he deserved another chance, that sort of thing.'

'He backed a wrong 'un there,' Shap said.

'Urwin was mouthing off outside the inquest,' Richard said.

'So Howard Urwin could have got the gun from Matthews two years ago?' Janine weighed this up. 'He hangs onto it then suddenly wants vengeance and hey presto he is armed and dangerous and ready to go?' She shook her head, it was iffy.

'Matthews could have stashed it before his arrest,' Shap said. He's released and then Uncle Howard asks him for a favour when Doc Halliwell gets off scot free.'

'Urwin asks Matthews to do the deed?' Richard said.

'Or lend him the gun,' Shap said.

'Matthews keeps insisting he's gone straight,' Lisa said.

'Well, he would,' Shap said, 'It could have been Adele Young out for blood — on the house to house reports she was seen in the area on Tuesday.'

'She lives in the area,' Butchers said.

'Here,' Shap found the reference, 'seen out in the vicinity, just before half-six.'

Janine felt her pulse quicken. 'Close to the time of the attack. That gives us motive, means and opportunity.' She went up to the boards, drew a line to connect one side, one line of inquiry, to the other.

'We thought it was either a gang crime or something linked to the practice,' Janine said, 'maybe it's a bit of both: the motive's a vengeful patient or their relative — Adele Young or Howard Urwin — but the gang link, in the shape of Matthews, supplies the weapon.'

'It's personal not business,' Richard said.

'Shall we bring her in, boss?' Butchers offered.

'I'll go and talk to her first,' Janine said, 'I still think this runs counter to her crusade for legal redress.'

'Urwin might favour different tactics,' Shap said.

'Yes. Someone for Howard Urwin?' Janine said. Butchers got to his feet. 'Not you, Butchers. You're still on the files. Shap?'

Shap nodded.

Butchers sat down heavily, Janine knew he was missing the action, probably feeling sidelined, shunted off combing through the paperwork at the surgery but Janine knew that methodical work was often critical — and Butchers was good at it.

'Urwin works for a floor cleaning company, they operate out of the Portwood industrial estate,' Lisa said.

'Nice work, Lisa,' Janine said.

'What's with the long face?' Shap said to Butchers as he made to leave. 'You love it there. You're like a wasp in jam. Got your feet under the desk, surrounded by women.'

'Piss off,' Butchers said.

'It's that Vicky Stonnall, she's the one, isn't she?' Shap said. 'Bet you're dying for her to take your temperature.'

Janine turned away stifling a laugh as Butchers' face flooded with red.

CHAPTER 27

Janine went to see Adele Young on her own, preferring a softly-softly approach. The woman had lost her only child and the man she held accountable for the death of her daughter had been cleared of any wrongdoing. She must be hurt, angry. But angry enough to turn to violence?

The surgery straddled two communities. On the leafier side was a haven for professionals and also bohemian types. You'd have to be a professional, have a well-paid job to afford a mortgage in those parts. Across the far side of the main road, was a council estate, most of it still rented out as social housing.

Adele Young's house, on the estate, looked well-kept but spartan from the outside, no hanging baskets or garden tubs as there were in the adjoining property. No time for any of that, Janine imagined, all Adele Young's energy swallowed up by the campaign for justice for Marcie.

Adele answered the door and Janine showed her ID. 'I'm DCI Lewis, Greater Manchester Police, can I come in?'

'What for?' Adele said. Her black hair was cut short, there were dark shadows under her eyes and her lips were chapped, peeling.

'I'm leading the investigation into the murder of Dr Halliwell,' Janine said.

'And?' Adele's arms were crossed, the hostility clear on her face.

'And I would like to ask you a few questions.'

'We've already had your lot knocking on the door,' Adele Young said. 'I told them I hadn't seen anything.'

'I would still like to talk to you.' Janine held her gaze and eventually Adele Young turned and walked inside leaving Janine to follow.

In the living room, a coffee table was covered with papers, cuttings and files, material for Adele's campaign. There were photos of Marcie all around the room; as a toddler with an enormous stuffed rabbit, a schoolgirl with her hair in corn-rows, a teenager dressed up for a big event. Janine thought fleetingly of Eleanor, tried to imagine her getting addicted to drugs, overdosing.

'I was sorry to hear about your daughter. You thought Dr Halliwell was wrong, the way he dealt with her. There was an incident when you challenged him about that?'

'Yeah, that's right,' she said.

'You were abusive?' Janine said.

The woman's lips tightened. 'I was at my wit's end. Close to locking her up to stop her going off and getting what she needed and he wouldn't listen. All he could do was pontificate about his own bloody opinion. I'm watching her fall apart because he's cut the dose so much, and he didn't get it. You bet I lost it,' her voice shook. 'I could see what was going to happen . . . I knew . . . and I couldn't save her.' Tears sprang into her eyes. 'God, I miss her. You do your best to try and keep them safe . . .' her voice trailed off. She rubbed at her upper arms as if she was trying to warm herself.

'And then the inquest, too, that must have been hard,' Janine said.

'You've no idea,' Adele said simply.

'I am sorry,' Janine said. 'Adele, I need to ask you where you were on Tuesday evening, between six and seven?'

Adele stared at her, eyes shrewd, mouth twisting. 'Piss off,' she said.

'I need you to answer the question,' Janine said.

Adele Young gave a shake of her head.

'Adele, I'm sorry, I need to rule you out of our inquiries and I can't do that if you won't cooperate.'

'Here,' Adele said.

'Alone?'

'With Howard.'

'All of the time?' Janine said.

'Yes.'

'The thing is, someone saw you on Tuesday, on the high street. Just before half-past six.'

'I've had enough of this. Do you think gunning someone down is the sort of justice I want for my daughter? Get out.' She stood up, flung her arm towards the door.

'Where were you going, Adele?'

'Get out. I'm not having you accuse me of stuff. Don't you think—' The woman stopped, trembling, close to breaking down. 'Just get out. Or arrest me if you think I shot him.'

CHAPTER 28

Shap approached the empty showroom and could see Howard Urwin inside cleaning the tiles with one of those large round polishing machines. He was a big bloke, looked like he worked out. Shap hated that whole scene; preferred his criminals underfed and feeble, physically incompetent, ideally with rickets too. But this vogue for body-building had everyone pumping iron and bulking up like they were all Rambos in the making.

Shap went in, he knew Urwin had seen him but the man still took his own sweet time turning the machine off.

'Howard Urwin?' Shap said. The man gave a nod, wary. Shap pointed to the floor, 'You missed a bit there.'

Urwin was not amused. Shap showed his ID. 'DS Shap. Your nephew Aaron Matthews, you done any business with him recently? He lend you anything?'

Howard Urwin gave a snort and switched his machine back on. *Prat.*

Shap walked over and flipped the switch at the socket. The machine whined to a halt.

'You weren't very happy with the inquest verdict, were you? Saw you mouthing off on the telly. Quite a temper you've got there,' Shap said.

'What do you want?' Urwin said.

'Where were you on Tuesday, between the hours of six and seven pm?'

'Home,' Urwin said, his eyes hooded.

Anyone corroborate that?' Shap said.

'Adele.'

'Either of you leave the house at all?' Shap said.

'Why?' Howard Urwin said.

'Because that's when someone took a pop at Dr Halliwell, three pops, to be exact,' Shap said, 'and you and the good doctor hadn't exactly parted on friendly terms.'

The man rolled back his shoulders, thought for a minute.

'Adele nipped out for milk, that's all,' Urwin said.

'When?'

'About six,' Urwin said.

'Where d'you get your milk?'

'Spar shop on the high street.'

* * *

Stonewalled by Adele, Janine went back to the office. Shap had rung in with Urwin's claim that Adele had gone out for milk. Janine sent Lisa to collect security camera footage from the store, for the time in question. And if it didn't prove Howard Urwin's account? If Adele had been elsewhere at that crucial time, perhaps heading for the surgery . . . Her job was to follow the evidence, Janine knew that, wherever it led. To be objective about it but she hoped to hell that Adele Young hadn't gone and done something she'd regret for the rest of her life.

CHAPTER 29

Roy polished his shoes. They really needed re-heeling but they'd have to do. He had hung up his suit and shirt and tie, all ready.

The bed had gone now and the medicines, Peggy's inhalers too, so the room looked bare, just his chair and the side table there.

He had been up to Cooper's with the clothes for Peggy: her navy dress — the one with the flowers pattern — and her miraculous medal and rosary beads and her wedding ring all to be buried with her.

The flowers he had chosen were a mix of roses: red, white and yellow with some ferns and gypsophilia. Peggy loved roses, she had grown them in the little garden at the back of the house, different varieties, so there was always something in bloom. She'd spend hours out there, pruning or deadheading, tying in and cutting flowers for the house.

As was the custom, her body would be taken to church that evening in preparation for the requiem mass the following day.

He got out the photograph albums. Peggy had put them together. Three leather-bound books full of the best pictures they had taken of Simon, as a baby, as he grew, holidays, birthday parties, playing on his bike.

Roy didn't need to open them, all those pictures were vivid in his mind. Simon on his shoulders, in Peggy's arms, Simon covered in ice cream, in school uniform, with his first skateboard, on his eighteenth birthday. The picture they had used for his funeral.

Roy took the albums outside and got the barbecue lighter fuel, poured it over them and set the lot alight. The flames flashed high, scorching some of the rose bushes then subsided as the books burned to ash.

He wrote a letter then, brief and to the point, and found a stamp for it in the drawer in the kitchen. Second class. That would do. He didn't feel the need to explain himself but he knew that Peggy would want him to set the record straight. He ought to take responsibility for his actions. If everyone did that, then things would not have got to this state in the first place.

He drew a chit of paper from his pocket, checking that he'd not forgotten anything that had to be done.

Satisfied, he looked outside. It was just beginning to spit so he put his coat on and set off to the post box down the road.

He ached with fatigue, wanted nothing more than to sleep. But it would soon all be over.

CHAPTER 30

Lisa was running the security film from the Spar shop, the shop floor was visible, the entrance door in the centre. Janine watched as the digital clock on the film clicked up close to six o'clock.

'She's a real fighter,' Janine said to Richard, 'I can't believe it's her.'

'You can't deny she was out for Halliwell's blood,' he said.

'Yes, but she's shouting it from the rooftops, taking it to the highest authority, whipping up debate — that's not the sort of person who then turns round and performs a vigilante execution.' Janine gestured to the screen. 'There she is.'

They watched as Adele got a two litre bottle of milk from the chiller and paid at the counter.

'But which way does she go now?' Janine said. She held her breath as Adele exited the shop. Released it when she saw her turn left.

'Away from the surgery — towards home,' Lisa said.

Janine was relieved and Richard dipped his head, acknowledged her hunch had been right.

Janine signalled to the 'grudge' list on the boards.

'Right, let's try and eliminate some more of these names.'

* * *

Next on Shap's list was Mr Neville Pemberton, an address in the pricey part of the area. When Shap reached it he found the smart semi had been adapted. A disabled ramp wound up to the front door where there was an entry phone. Shap pressed the buzzer.

'Who is it?'

'DS Shap, Greater Manchester Police. Can I have a word with you Mr Pemberton?'

'You're having one, aren't you?'

Smart arse. 'In person,' Shap said.

'What's it about?'

'Serious crime. You've heard about Dr Halliwell?' Shap said.

'He won't be doing any more damage, now, will he?'

'Please can you open the door, sir? Now.'

There was a buzzing noise and Shap pushed the door back in time to see Pemberton in a wheelchair, half-way down the hall by the entry phone unit. He was obviously very frail.

'You made an official complaint?' Shap said.

Pemberton made a noise of disgust. 'Flu,' he gestured to himself. 'This look like flu to you? Meningitis and he failed to spot it.'

'Where were you yesterday evening between six and seven?' Shap said.

The man burst out laughing. 'Seriously?' he said.

'If you could answer the question?' Shap did not like being jerked about.

'Here. Arguing the toss about my disabled living allowance. Then at the pub,' Pemberton said.

'Can anyone verify that?' Shap said.

'My personal carer might, she's the poor sod had to get me dressed and into the Ring and Ride. Now, it's going to take me the best part of fifteen minutes to get back to the computer so unless there's anything else . . .'

'Your carer's name?' Shap said.

'Oh, for fuck's sake,' Pemberton said.

Shap waited, pen poised. Pemberton spat out the details and when Shap got through to her, the carer confirmed Pemberton's alibi.

CHAPTER 31

It still felt unreal to Norma, impossible to truly believe. The nearest she could come when she attempted to think about it was, who on earth would shoot Don? Perhaps it was a mistake or an accident, Don was just in the wrong place at the wrong time. Nothing else made sense. It was all so random, life — wasn't it? If she'd not got that puncture, not met Don, if they'd not lost the baby, then everything would have been different. She wouldn't be here now. He wouldn't be dead. If the baby had lived . . .

'You will have another,' that's what people said when you lost a baby, had a miscarriage or a stillbirth. 'Nature's way.' Norma hated that platitude. Nature's way was brutal and whimsical, cruel. The baby had been perfect. Everyone agreed. Perfect but dead.

She felt as though her heart had been taken from her. Birthed and disposed of, like the stillborn child had been, like the placenta. Taken in a mess of pain and blood and grief. Don at her side, grey faced and stoic, held her hand and rubbed her back and when it came to pushing called her a good girl, just like the midwives did. They'd induced her, so labour came on swift and savage, cresting pains robbing her of breath and sense and the ability to speak. When the baby was born there was only silence in the room.

Norma didn't want to look, didn't want to see, imagined gross deformities, something bestial. The midwife said gently, 'It's a little girl.' And Norma's eyes flew to the form on the plastic sheeting. And she was perfect.

'I am sorry,' the midwife said, 'you get your breath and then we'll see about the third stage.' And with that she folded the sheet over the baby and took her away.

'Why?' Norma said to Don. 'The cord, it wasn't around her neck.'

'No,' he said, his voice husky, 'sometimes we never know.'

And they never did.

Norma was able to go home the following day, away from the ward of newborns and happy mothers.

And into the pit.

That's how she always thought it. Buried in the dark and cold. Numb and unfeeling.

Don still had to work and study. Some days she didn't move from her bed from the time he left the house until he returned. There were days when speech was too much effort. She took the tablets that had helped settle her nerves at university but they weren't strong enough. Food was irrelevant, sickening. She didn't bathe unless Don insisted, running her bath, taking her rancid clothes away.

He tried talking to her but the words slithered around her and sank, joining her in the pit.

She took lots of tablets once and Don found her, her face and hair spackled with vomit. He raged at her. He thought she'd meant to kill herself.

'No,' she said, 'I just wanted to feel safe again. The tablets, they're not strong enough. You don't have to stay. I'm not well, I know that. And now . . .' Without the baby, she meant.

'I'm staying,' he said, 'you'll get better.' He was so determined.

He filled a prescription, came home with it and emphasized it was just for the short term, to help her through this rough patch. It helped. It took away the cold, hard grief and it filled the gaping hole where her heart had been. It helped her forget about the baby. About everything. She began to live again.

CHAPTER 32

It was an honest mistake Lisa kept telling herself but what if DI Mayne wouldn't give her a second chance? She wanted to be a detective, she liked the work, thought she could be good at it, or could be if she hadn't made such an idiotic mistake.

She looked in the mirror, straightened her back, lowered her shoulders. Time to go.

When she knocked on his door he called her in.

'Shut the door,' he said and her heart sank. His tone was cold, he looked pissed off. She stood to attention in front of his desk.

'Put yourself in my shoes,' he said, 'a fundamental mistake, what action do you expect me to take?'

'Demotion,' Lisa said, 'back to the beat, filing.'

'That might be appropriate but I'm not going to do that. Instead I want you to revise all your arrest and caution procedure. . .'

He was giving her a chance. Yes! She felt the weight lifting, the dread melting away.'

'. . . You study your handbook. In future, if there are diversions, interruptions of any sort, you double check that you've actioned and noted every single step. Clear?'

'Yes, sir. Thank you.' She wanted to smile, fought to keep her face set, serious.

'You stay on the case,' DI Mayne said, 'and you see it through. You deal with the fact that if Aaron Matthews is guilty, he may well escape prosecution as a result of your oversight. If that turns out to be the case you can explain it to Norma Halliwell in person.'

'Yes, sir,' Lisa said, praying that it wouldn't come to that, but prepared to do whatever he said as long as she could stay on the team.

* * *

Butchers had continued to speak to patients who had seen Dr Halliwell on the day he died to see if anyone remembered anything out of the ordinary, or noticed anything sinister. Now and again he consulted with Vicky who knew a good deal about the practice even though she had only been receptionist for a couple of years.

'The home visits,' Butchers asked her. 'Dr Halliwell called on Roy Gant on Tuesday.'

'Oh, yes. His wife Peggy, she'd been ill a while. A smoker — she had emphysema and heart trouble then they found the cancer.'

'So, it was expected — her death.'

'Yeah. Poor bloke. Be nice,' Vicky said.

'I'm always nice,' Butchers said. His phone rang — the boss calling. Vicky left him to it.

'Boss?' Butchers said.

'Listen, Shap's not got anywhere so far with those who've made official complaints. We are still investigating the link between Howard Urwin and Aaron Matthews in case Matthews acted on Urwin's behalf. Adele and Howard Urwin are alibi-ing each other but I'm convinced that Adele wouldn't countenance the killing.'

Butchers slipped off his shoes and stepped onto the scales.

'So Aaron Matthews is still the lead horse?' Butchers said.

'That's right but we continue other lines of inquiry and I'm thinking there could be patients who weren't happy with Dr Halliwell but who won't necessarily have filed an official complaint. They might just have jumped ship, moved to another practice, sacked him. So look at anyone who left his list in the last few years; changed their doctor. There may be something there, below the radar.'

Butchers stepped off the scales and looked at the BMI chart on the wall. His reading put him firmly in the 'obese' category.

'Will do.'

'How are you getting on with the appointments?' the boss said.

Speak to your GP about lifestyle change and weight reduction. 'I've talked to all the afternoon surgery appointments from Tuesday and there's nothing there,' Butchers said. 'It's like Dr Finlay's casebook, not a bad word from any of them, the man's a saint. Thought I'd do the home visits next, confirm the timing?'

'Who were they?'

Butchers picked up his notes from the desk. 'Marjorie Keysham, she's in a nursing home, Halliwell prescribed diamorphine for her. He also called to certify the cause of Peggy Gant's death, she died at home after an illness, husband's name is Roy.'

'Shap can try Keysham, if she's up to having visitors — send him the details. You check with Roy Gant,' the boss said.

* * *

Shap hated places like this. All floral curtains and the smell of piss under air-freshener. A load of old women with grey perms and twin-sets. And now the ones he was talking to, treating him like an idiot.

He repeated, 'Dr Halliwell came on Tuesday afternoon, he left a prescription for you.'

Both of the old biddies, Marjorie Keysham and the Matron, shook their heads, acting like he was the one with missing marbles.

'Tuesday afternoon, diamorphine for Marjorie Keysham.' Maybe it needed repeating a few times to permeate, Shap thought.

'I was here,' the Matron said, 'we had no visit from Dr Halliwell.'

'And Tuesday, I go to my reading group,' Marjorie Keysham said. 'Besides, I'd remember if I'd seen the doctor, especially if he'd given me morphine. Fantastic stuff, had it when I broke my hip. I'd remember, Sergeant: I've got cancer not dementia.'

Both of them bounced their heads up and down like two nodding dogs.

Had Butchers got it arse over tit or had Dr Halliwell been playing hooky? Pretending he was off on home visits when he was actually on the golf course or screwing some bit on the side. Something was going on.

Shap explained the situation to Butchers who got all excited about it, something to do with the prescriptions. He told Shap to come to the surgery and said the boss would want to be in on it too.

* * *

When they had all arrived, Butchers showed them the pattern he'd found: a list of patients, all with addresses at nursing homes, all with prescriptions for diamorphine.

'I've rung three of them,' he said, 'and it's the same story. Halliwell has invented these visits and then he's written the prescriptions.'

'Always diamorphine? Always nursing homes?' the boss said.

'Yes,' Butchers said.

'Marjorie Keysham's prescription was cashed in by Halliwell at Picket's pharmacy, near the nursing home,' Shap said. 'The pharmacy say it's not uncommon for a GP to pop in with prescriptions. But the actual prescription was for three times the amount that Halliwell entered on the computer records when he got back to work.'

'And no-one compares the two amounts?' Richard said.

'Apparently not,' Shap said. 'The only way he'd be found out is if another doctor got called out to the patient, and discovered there'd been no visit, and they'd not had any medicine. Like I did.'

'What about the drugs budget,' the boss said, 'that must have been on the high side?'

'If he's been at it for years then it might not be that obvious,' Richard said.

'What was Halliwell doing with the drugs?' the boss said.

'Flogging them,' Shap said.

'Who to?' the boss said. 'Find that out and maybe that will lead us to his murderer.'

CHAPTER 33

Back in the incident room, Janine was trying to work out a narrative that fit the evidence to date using Richard as her sounding board. 'Halliwell and Aaron Matthews were known to each other, Halliwell was his GP. We know Halliwell was stealing drugs and we also know Matthews' gun killed him. Add in Matthews' history . . .'

'A drug deal gone sour?' Richard said.

'It's a possibility,' Janine said. 'And our Dr Halliwell is not exactly the upstanding pillar of the community we thought he was.'

'Boss. I've got the Range Rover, Monday.'

Lisa had been scrolling through CCTV footage of traffic on the high street for Monday and Tuesday evening looking for the Range Rover.

She lined up the footage and played it for them to watch it driving down the high street from the west and then turning off out of view, towards the surgery.'

'Ten to six,' Lisa said. 'That's the only one that matches Dr Gupta's description, and the time's right.'

'Tenner says it's a knock-off job,' Shap said, 'the gang will have used it to run a recce, done the job, then torched it.'

'The job being to steal Halliwell's briefcase and the diamorphine?' Janine said. 'I don't know. Yes, the doctor is stealing drugs but the overall amount is chicken feed, a gang dealing in drugs is going to want a much bigger consignment.'

'Maybe we are back to a splinter group,' Richard said, 'youngsters flexing their muscles.'

'Or Aaron Matthews is a junkie and somehow finds out he can rip off his family doctor for the goods,' Shap said.

'How would he find out,' Janine said, 'we've only just stumbled on it. It's obviously been the good doctor's secret for a considerable time.'

Lisa shrugged, 'I wouldn't have said Matthews was a junkie.'

'Tell by looking, can you?' Shap said.

'Nothing to show that at his flat, no obvious physical signs,' Lisa said.

'And Tuesday?' Janine said, gesturing to the screen.

'Nothing,' Lisa said, 'this vehicle wasn't in the area anywhere close to the time of the shooting — not on the tapes and it would have had to pass this camera to reach the surgery.'

Janine sighed, finding the car in the vicinity on the Monday but not on the Tuesday was disappointing.

'Can we get the plate?' Richard nodded at the frozen image of the Range Rover.

Lisa wound the tape until the vehicle could be seen from the front and zoomed in. 'Check it for registered keeper.'

'It'll be a knock off,' Shap repeated.

Lisa accessed the database and typed in the registration number. The screen loaded with the registered owner details.

'Neil Langan?' Richard said.

Janine felt a kick in her chest. 'Langan? We've a Dawn Langan. Practice nurse.'

'Same address?' Janine asked.

Shap checked Dawn's details. 'Yes.'

'What was Mr Langan doing lurking outside his wife's place of work on Monday?' Janine said.

'Well, he wasn't giving her a lift home,' Richard said.

'Butchers said Dawn was a bit off with him,' Shap told them, 'hiding something? She must be sweating cobs.'

Janine rang Butchers at the surgery and explained the situation. Tasked him with speaking to Dawn Langan and establishing her husband's whereabouts.

* * *

'Dawn, can I have a word?' Butchers said. 'It's actually Neil I hoped to talk to. Is he at home?'

'No,' she froze.

'At work?'

'No.'

Butchers waited. Dawn's eyes flicked all over the place.

'Is that usual?' Butchers said, 'Him being off the radar?'

She looked like she'd break, trembling, her chin wobbling, ponytail shivering.

'Where is he, Dawn?' Butchers said gently.

'I don't know where he is,' she blurted out, 'he's not been into the sorting office. And his phone's off.'

'Was he at home in the early hours of Tuesday morning?' Butchers said, thinking about the attack on Halliwell's car.

Dawn looked away, as if she daren't meet Butchers eyes. 'No,' she whispered.

'What about Tuesday evening, around six thirty?'

She didn't answer. Butchers could hear her breath, jerky and uneven.

'And you didn't think to tell us?' Butchers said. *Missing at the time of the murder.* 'Why's that then?' He picked up his phone.

'Because this is nothing to do with him,' she said vehemently, 'even if he found out about us, he'd never hurt anybody. Neil is not a murderer. No way.'

'Whoah!' Butchers said, 'Stop right there.' *Found out about us?* 'Who's 'us'?

Dawn Langan burst into tears. It was a good five minutes before Butchers could get any sense out of her. And when he did the whole picture changed.

CHAPTER 34

They were searching for Neil Langan: using the automatic number plate recognition system to look for sightings of his car, following procedures to get access to his phone records, and liaising with his bank so they could track him when he used his cards.

'So,' Shap marvelled, 'Dawn Langan and Don Halliwell, playing doctors and nurses.'

'And when Neil Langan finds out . . .' Janine said.

'He smashes up Halliwell's car . . .' Shap said.

'And then shoots him,' Richard said.

It was a strong motive and Janine knew that jealousy was a very powerful emotion. Being betrayed, cuckolded, dumped, drove people to kill. A minority to be sure — otherwise the murder rate would be phenomenal. She remembered her own sense of shock when she caught Pete cheating, the numbness giving way to a mix of cold fury and deep sadness. That Pete could risk it all, their marriage, their life as a family, daily contact with his children, for the thrill of sex. Janine was hurt even more when Pete chose Tina and left Janine, who was expecting their fourth child, on her own.

She had fantasized about hurting him, humiliating him, called down all sorts of catastrophes and punishments but that was all they were.

So, had Neil Langan, a postman married to the practice nurse, a man with no criminal record, been driven to act with such brutality? Violence against property was a very different matter than violence against the person. What had he thought? That if he shot Halliwell, put him out of action, that he might be able to win back his errant wife? Hardly. Janine imagined that if Langan had killed Halliwell it would've been done in a blur of hatred and rage, with no thought of the far-reaching consequences of his actions.

'He just happens to carry a handgun in his postie's bag?' Janine said. 'He goes from a clean sheet to criminal damage and murder in twenty four hours?'

'He's there on the Monday, casing the joint, planning it,' Shap said.

'Then why bother with smashing up the car, if you're going to kill someone anyway . . .' Janine said.

'Maybe the car was the initial plan and then he's still mad with jealousy so he ups the ante,' Shap said.

'Why the wait?' Janine said. 'The car was smashed up in the early hours then he waits all day until the surgery is closing to make his move on Halliwell. What's that about?'

'Perhaps that's the only time he can get Halliwell on his own,' said Richard.

'We don't have the Range Rover in the area on the Tuesday evening,' Janine said.

Shap shrugged. 'Went on foot, less easy to trace him.'

Lisa called out, 'Boss, Langan used his card on Tuesday at a Travel Inn at Chester services.'

'He'll be long gone, now,' Shap said.

'No, he used the same card at the ATM there last night,' Lisa said.

'Go on, then,' Janine told them, 'what you waiting for?'

* * *

Butchers was trying to establish whether Halliwell had actually been to visit Roy Gant or if that was another cover story for this funny business with the drugs.

Gant lived in a small terrace with mullioned windows, double glazed so they looked odd, too fussy for the property, Butchers thought.

Butchers knocked and introduced himself. He apologized for the intrusion and explained the reason for his call.

Roy Gant grunted and nodded he should go on. He was dishevelled, Butchers saw, probably still dazed from his wife's death.

'Mr Gant, did Dr Halliwell visit you on Tuesday afternoon?'

'Yes, that's right. He had to do the cause of death certificate, for Peggy. Then he was calling home, he said, before afternoon surgery.'

This was news to Butchers.

'What time was he here?' Butchers said.

'About two o'clock,' Gant said.

'How long was he here?'

'About ten, fifteen minutes. Just filling out the certificate,' Gant's voice caught. Butchers nodded, a little uneasy at the man's raw grief.

There was nothing about Dr Halliwell calling to his own home in his schedule for the Tuesday but maybe something like that wasn't out of the ordinary. Dr Halliwell was in charge of the practice after all. If he fancied nipping home for a bite to eat or forty winks he'd not have to answer to anyone.

Butchers thanked Mr. Gant and back in his car he jotted down the new timeline.

1.30 p.m., Chemist's — collecting drugs for Marjorie Keysham
2.00 p.m. Roy Gant's
2.20 p.m. Home

What if Halliwell was an addict? Maybe he popped home to use the drugs? The notion struck Butchers like a stroke of genius for all of ten seconds. It wouldn't work, would it? They would have checked at the post mortem.

CHAPTER 35

Lisa and Shap enquired at the Travel Inn reception for Neil Langan and the receptionist pointed them towards the lounge bar.

'It could be a domestic after all,' Lisa said. And if it was, if Neil Langan had killed Halliwell in a crime of passion, then Lisa would be off the hook for messing up the Matthews arrest.

Shap just rolled his eyes, like she was baying for the moon.

Neil Langan was slumped in a corner booth, eyes shut, empty glasses in front of him.

'Neil Langan?' Shap said.

Langan startled awake, eyes bleary. 'What?'

'DS Shap and DC Goodall.' Shap made the introductions.

Neil Langan stretched his neck, as though he'd a crick in it. 'I wondered how long you'd be,' he said. 'I thought she should know that's all.' He gave a shrug.

'Back up a bit, sir,' Lisa said. 'You were outside the surgery where your wife works on Monday night?'

'Yes,' Neil Langan said, 'I wanted to see with my own eyes. I'd rung the Monday before to ask Dawn something, but the surgery was closed.' He gave a bitter laugh. 'She wasn't at a late-night clinic every Monday like she told me; she was shagging Don Halliwell.' He leaned forward and lifted a glass, whisky, Lisa guessed, and drained it. 'I waited this time,' Langan went on, 'and I followed them to the hotel. Then I got hammered and I rang Mrs Halliwell and I told her all about them. Then I sank a few more — pints and chasers.' He waved the glass. 'And I went round there in the middle of the night and I rammed his car. Bastard.'

No attempt to mislead them or deny any of it.

'Where were you on Tuesday, afternoon and evening?' Lisa said.

'Here,' Neil Langan said, 'well, that table over there, I think.' He flapped a hand. 'Or that one.'

'Can anyone confirm that?' Shap said.

'Ask the staff,' Neil Langan said. 'I'm their big spender, this week.' He waved at the bartender who gave a small shake of the head and busied himself stocking up the bottles behind, clearly weary of Langan, Lisa thought. She walked over to him and asked how long Langan had been in residence.

'Too long,' the man said.

'Do you know when he arrived?'

'He was in here as soon as we opened on Tuesday morning,' he said, 'drowning his sorrows.'

'Did he leave the premises any time on Tuesday?'

'No. Still here when I clocked off at seven,' the man said.

There was no way Neil Langan could have returned to Manchester and shot the doctor.

Lisa went back across to the booth and got there in time to hear Langan protesting, 'I don't know what you're wasting time with me for — it's Norma Halliwell you want to be talking to. I tell her what's going on, that her husband is shagging my wife, and next thing . . .' He mimed someone shooting a gun, made a *pow* sound like a kid might. 'I'd no idea she'd take it like that, shoot her own husband. That's who you should be talking to.' He stared at the empty glass in his hand, held it up to the light as if there might be more booze hiding somewhere inside it. 'You should be talking to her. I spill the beans and she goes mental. Norma Halliwell. Unbelievable.'

CHAPTER 36

Janine and Richard were on their way to the Halliwell house. Janine was trying to accommodate the new theory, relinquish Langan as a suspect given his watertight alibi and focus on Norma Halliwell. 'She might have motive but how on earth would she get hold of a gun? She's a piano teacher — her clientele aren't likely to be toting small arms about,' Janine said.

'Hit man?' Richard said.

'I can't see it, though I have been known to be wrong.'

'Steady on,' Richard said.

She cut her eyes at him. 'A doctor's wife, in her sixties. Can you see her hanging round dodgy pubs in search of a contract killer? Not in a million years. She only learned about the affair on Monday night. And how did she get to the surgery and back? Halliwell had her car, his was wrecked.'

'Taxi?' Richard said.

'So how do we handle it?' Richard said as Janine drew the car into the kerb outside the house.

'We can't put the gun in her hand,' Janine said, 'but she's clearly been keeping things from us. Not a dicky bird about Langan's phone call. So let's push her a bit, see what we get, eh?'

* * *

Norma Halliwell took her time to answer the door and seemed unsurprised to find them there.

'We'd like a few minutes of your time,' Janine explained, 'to try and clarify some points that have come to light.'

Norma gave a nod and they went with her into the front room again.

She sat in an armchair, her manner distracted, absent, picking at the piping on the chair.

'Neil Langan rang you on Monday evening,' Janine said.

Norma glanced at Janine then lowered her eyes.

'He told you that Don was having a relationship with his wife, Dawn Langan,' Janine said. 'That must have been quite a shock?'

'Not really,' Norma said, 'I thought there was someone.'

'Did you talk to Don about it?'

'No,' she said.

'You failed to mention it to us,' Richard said.

Norma shook her head, 'It didn't mean anything.'

'Has it happened before?' Janine said.

'Probably,' Norma sounded tired. 'I don't ask.'

'You must have suspected that Neil Langan was behind the damage to the car.' There was an edge of disbelief in Richard's tone, 'possibly involved in your husband's death, and you still said nothing.'

Norma let her hands fall into her lap. 'When they told me he was dead, I just couldn't think,' she said. Then something occurred to her and she straightened up, frowning, and said, 'Mr Langan — he didn't do it, did he? Surely not?' Sounding innocent herself, Janine thought, or was she outwitting them?

'No,' Richard said.

'Is there anything else you haven't told us about, Mrs Halliwell?' Janine said.

'No.'

'Where were you between six and seven on Tuesday evening?'

Norma Halliwell stared at her, pain lancing through her eyes, then gave a hollow laugh, incredulous. 'Here. I was teaching.'

'We could verify that?' Richard said.

'Yes,' she said.

'When did you last see your husband?' Janine said.

'When he left for work on Tuesday,' Norma said.

Wearily Norma Halliwell provided them with the two phone numbers for the pupils who had come for lessons on Tuesday evening, one at six and one at half past.

Out in the car, Richard made the calls and got confirmation from the parents involved.

CHAPTER 37

They never knew what had happened to the baby after the midwife had wrapped her in the sheet and left the room. The post-mortem, of course, a futile attempt to find a reason for the death but after that? Burial in some common grave, disposal like so much medical waste? In recent years, other couples affected like them had searched for their lost children, named them, had services and created memorials. The modern view was that acknowledging the life lost was a healthy response. But it held no sway with Don when she raised it, he regarded it as an indulgence at best and opening wounds at worst. She let it be.

They would never have another child. She hadn't realized at first, couples were advised to avoid pregnancy too soon, so when she had clambered out of the pit and they began making love again she had gone on the pill, a new version. As the months went by her mother began to drop hints. 'Don't leave it too long,' she said, 'if you're worried about the risks—'

'I know the risks,' Norma had said, 'we just want to be more settled, it's a hard year for Don.'

Don told her if they wanted to try again, she'd have to stop the medication, it would harm the baby. Even the thought of that, going a day without it, let alone nine whole months, made her feel panicky, a fluttering feeling in her chest, her mouth dry and her face hot.

'Not yet,' she said, 'I'm not ready.'

Thankfully, Don didn't seem desperate to have children unlike some men who wanted to make sure the family line continued. They discussed it on occasion back then, it was always Don who raised the issue. And then one time, just after he'd started his own practice, she had said, in response to his asking if she'd thought any more about babies, that she was happy as they were, just the two of them; that she didn't think she could ever face another pregnancy after what happened. She'd taken a steadying breath, saying, 'If a family is important to you then maybe we should think about separation.'

'Norma,' he said, looking exasperated and her stomach turned over. Then his expression softened. 'You idiot. It's you I want, first and foremost. That's what matters most. The family, well . . .' he shrugged, '. . . it might be nice but . . . I wouldn't be the one dealing with it all and . . . it's just not that important.'

'You're sure?' She had stared at him.

'Yes,' he said.

She was so grateful. She ran the house and began to teach piano and went to parties with Don's friends from work. In time as their friends had children, the friendships weakened and withered. They didn't really need other people.

* * *

I was hiding, Norma thought, I've been hiding my whole life. Don had his work, his patients, his colleagues, his mistresses. And I had Don. Like Sleeping Beauty. But Norma's prince had not woken her with a kiss, he pricked her with a needle, kept her drugged and docile and safe. Oh, yes, he tried to wean her off, now and again, but she felt that was to protect himself as much as anything. If it ever came out, he'd be disbarred.

The thought of relief brought saliva into her mouth, a lifting of the fear that gripped the back of her neck. But what about tomorrow, a voice in her head murmured. And the next day and the next? How long can you go on?

It was over. Don knew that, that was probably why he was still here, whispering her name, waiting in the corners where the shadows fell. He knew what was best. Always had. She was tired of hiding, exhausted by the fear of the future. Yes, she might last another three days but then what? The pit waiting to suck her back in. Or hospitalisation?

Outside, the aspens sighed in the wind and the house creaked in reply.

There was nothing else to do. No one to tell. Norma climbed upstairs and got things ready. She lay on the bed, let out a sigh.

'Norma,' he said.

'I know,' she answered, 'I'm coming.'

She tried to think about the happy times, that first coffee with him, their honeymoon in Edinburgh, the happiness of easy routine and affection and comfort, of restyling the house and pouring her love into it. Don never left the house without kissing her goodbye. The wind blew again, stronger, so she felt the house shaking. Was that possible?

'Norma.'

She couldn't wait any longer. It was time to go.

CHAPTER 38

The case kept shifting shape, Janine thought, every time they believed a line of inquiry was gaining legs, something would come along and kick them away, leaving them winded.

First they had the prospect of a robbery turned violent, then all the merry dance that Fraser McKee took them on, the hunt for a patient with a grudge, then Halliwell re-cast as a drug dealer, next the prospect of a crime of passion. And now, she thought, where are we now? What was solid?

'With Langan and Mrs Halliwell out of the picture where do we go?' she said to Richard as they drove towards the police station.

'Aaron Matthews is all we've got,' Richard said.

Janine rang Butchers. 'We've hit a brick wall with the jealous spouse angle,' she said.

'Maybe not,' Butchers said. 'Halliwell called at Roy Gant's at two o'clock but he told Gant he was going home before he went back to work. Perhaps things started going sour then.'

'Norma's just sworn to us that she last saw him in the morning,' Janine said.

'Unless Halliwell was lying to Roy Gant?' Butchers said.

'Why bother — why raise it at all?' Janine said. 'It's more likely she's lying to us. Again.'

Janine ended the call. 'Halliwell told Roy Gant he was calling home,' she said to Richard, 'you just heard her say she last saw him that morning. Why lie about that?'

'He comes home, she confronts him with the affair, he's not sorry enough, he taunts her, tells her he's leaving her maybe. She decides to punish him.'

'But she was here when he was shot,' Janine said.

'She had help?' Richard said.

'I don't know,' Janine said, 'but at the very least let's challenge her on the last sighting.'

* * *

There was no answer when Richard rang the bell again.

'Perhaps she hopes we'll go away if she leaves it long enough,' Janine said.

Richard walked down the steps and along to peer in the front room window.

'No sign,' he said,

Janine tried the windows at the side. She wasn't visible anywhere downstairs. Janine felt a chill inside. 'I don't like this,' she said, 'we need to get in there.'

She's not moving.

Richard didn't hesitate. When the front door wouldn't give under sustained kicks, he picked an edging stone out from the flower border and used it to smash through the stained-glass sidelight. He reached in and undid the latch.

Janine kept calling out, 'Mrs Halliwell? Norma?'

After double checking the ground floor, they took the stairs.

The master bedroom was at the front. She lay there on the bed, comatose, a band tied around her arm and sharps and ampoules on the bedside table.

'Oh, God,' Janine said. She picked up one of the ampoules and read the label. 'Diamorphine.'

Janine grabbed hold of the woman's shoulder, shook her hard, her head fell to the side. 'Can you hear me, Norma? Norma?'

Janine placed two fingers on the angle of the woman's jaw, felt a faint pulse in her neck and nodded to Richard who was already calling an ambulance.

'Now we know why Halliwell was stealing drugs,' Janine said.

'Help's on its way,' she said to Norma, 'there's an ambulance coming. You're going to be alright.'

She thought of Adele Young then, of her desperate battle to save Marcie. How many times had she found her daughter like this? And then to have finally got her help with Dr Halliwell, with the hope of being weaned off the heroin only to find that the dose reduction was too savage, was unbearable for the girl. Knowing that she would relapse, go in search of one more proper high, with deadly consequences.

CHAPTER 39

The hospital notified Janine when Norma was conscious and out of danger. Janine needed to talk to her, to try and establish if she had played any part in her husband's murder but she was also aware that Norma Halliwell was extremely vulnerable, grieving and suicidal. Had the police questioning prompted her attempt on her life? Had the suicide bid risen from guilt? And given she couldn't have pulled the trigger, that she was teaching at the time, was it possible she had engaged someone else to kill her husband?

A nurse was coming out of Norma's room as Janine arrived.

'She's still awake?' Janine checked and the nurse nodded.

Norma was sitting up in bed. Her eyes glanced at Janine then away again, indifferent.

'I'm sorry to disturb you,' Janine said, 'but there are questions I have to ask.'

The ethereal quality that Janine had noticed in Norma before seemed even more pronounced after her ordeal, her skin paper thin and porcelain white.

'Mrs Halliwell, can you tell me anything about what happened to your husband?'

'No,' Norma said.

'Are you sure about that?' Janine said.

She raised her eyes to meet Janine's. 'I could never hurt Don,' she said, 'he looked after me, I depended on him completely.'

'But the affair with his work colleague was a threat, and you got jealous?' Janine said.

'No,' Norma said, 'he'd never leave me, he loved me. She stroked the bed sheet, her long fingers pale, tapered, here and there a liver spot. 'You know, when they told me he was dead, the first thing I thought of, before anything else, was: how will I get my medication? The very first thing.' She made a little sound, breathy. 'I lost my husband and I lost my supplier too. I couldn't go on without him.'

'How long has this been going on, the drugs?' Janine said.

'Since we met practically. Every few years, Don would try and persuade me to go into rehabilitation but I couldn't face it. At medical school I'd needed stuff to keep me awake, stuff to help me sleep. I was always, strung out — I suppose. Then I got pregnant. We got married. But we lost the baby. Morphine made things bearable. Don helped me. And it got so there was no way back.'

'He enabled your addiction,' Janine said. 'As long as he was around, you didn't have to worry about it, deal with it.'

'So you see, I could never have hurt him — even if I had wanted to — because then I'd have no way of getting my medicine.' Tremors flickered in the muscles round her mouth.

Forty years, Janine thought, forty years of dependency. And the sheer hypocrisy of Halliwell. The same man who had kept his wife supplied with heroin had insisted on a rapid treatment plan for Marcie Young, against her family's wishes. Could that have been because he'd seen how persistent, persuasive addiction was first hand and feared Marcie would go the same way that Norma had? Or had he been rigid as a reaction against his complicity with Norma — compartmentalising his approach? Norma's addiction could be contained because she had money, access to safe drugs, privilege. Marcie's addiction killed her.

'What do I do now?' Norma Halliwell said, sounding lost. 'It's all gone.' She looked steadily at Janine, 'I wish you'd left me there,' she said.

Janine took a breath. 'People do it,' she said, 'they turn their lives around — it's not impossible.'

Norma turned away, her hands no longer smoothing the sheets but one set of nails digging into the flesh at the base of her thumb.

Norma Halliwell had been living in a cocoon, Janine thought as she walked along the corridor to the exit. A comfortable life as the doctor's wife, teaching piano and looking after the house. Respected, cosseted. Putting up with his dalliances because she had no option. It was a prison of sorts, trapped by her addiction. And the drug was the one true love of her life.

CHAPTER 40

Janine found Richard, Shap and Butchers at the pub, the two sergeants half way through a game of pool. They paused to hear what the trip to the hospital had produced.

Shap shook his head, mouth twisted. 'Who'd have pegged her for a junkie?' he said.

'You didn't see that one coming, did you, Shap?' Janine said. 'Me neither. Well, this time, Norma took the lot. She wasn't getting high, she was getting out.'

'Guilt?' Butchers said.

Janine shook her head. 'She'd never hurt him. No matter what she felt about the affair, all that really mattered to her was where her next fix was coming from. He was her source. No way would she jeopardise that.'

Shap nodded to Butchers and they returned to the pool table.

'No Lisa?' Janine said.

'She knows we're here,' Richard's tone was cool.

'Make her feel welcome, did you?' Janine said.

'Look, it's sorted,' he said. 'I spoke to her this afternoon. But until the case is cracked she doesn't know exactly how much damage she's done. She probably wants to see how it plays out.' He shrugged.

Janine studied him. 'You can come across as very harsh, you know?'

'Harsh? Hah! Harsh? You're calling me harsh? Is this a staff appraisal or what?' His eyes were gleaming, was he teasing her or spoiling for an argument? It wasn't how she would have managed the situation, coming down so heavily on Lisa. Lisa knew she'd made a mistake, a basic one and was obviously beating herself up about it. She would need to improve her performance, regain her reputation for being conscientious and reliable, which Janine believed her to be. But a cold shoulder from her line manager, exclusion from the inner circle of the team, was nothing less than petty. Janine wondered if there was anything else going on, other problems in Richard's life that were causing him stress and making him more judgmental. Teamwork was crucial to their job, to the possibility of success, and Janine prided herself on commanding the respect and loyalty of her troops but it could easily be jeopardized if schisms started appearing. She didn't feel now was the right time to go into it any more with Richard. She could only hope they got to solve the case because if Lisa's mistake put it out of reach then everything could collapse.

Richard was still looking at her. Janine held her hands up, letting it go.

Butchers potted the winning ball, shouting, 'Yes!' and Shap groaned with disgust.

'Doubles?' Butchers said.

Richard signalled to Janine and then to himself.

Janine picked up a cue.

'You break,' Shap said.

Janine took a sip of her drink and chalked her cue. 'If Norma Halliwell didn't shoot her husband, then who the hell did?' she said.

She lined up her sights and drew back the cue, hit the ball, breaking the triangle and potted a shot.

* * *

Janine waited until Tom had gone to bed to call Pete, Charlotte already down and Eleanor ensconced in her room. He actually picked up the phone. 'Can you come round now, we need to sort this out?'

'Bit tricky, I'm afraid, I've got Alfie.' He sounded pressured, like he was the only person in the world who had ever had to deal with a small baby. But she wasn't going to let him wriggle out of it.

'He is portable, isn't he?' Janine said, 'You've not superglued him to his cot? I'm in the rest of the evening.' She kept her tone frosty hoping he'd realise how pissed off she was and that he needed to face the music.

* * *

When Janine heard the door and went to answer it, Pete was there on his own. 'Managed to get him down,' Pete said.

'Good.'

They went in the kitchen, the scene of so many discussions, traumas and celebrations, throughout their married life.

'I need you to pull your weight with the kids. I end up making excuses for you. They don't want to hear it. I know Alfie wasn't exactly planned but it's not fair on our kids if you don't find a way of maintaining that contact. We knew it'd be a bit difficult when Alfie first arrived but he's two months old now. You need to make time for them as well.'

'It's not that easy—'

'I don't care, Pete. You promised me and you owe them. They don't need you any less because they're bigger.'

'I know,' he rubbed at his face. He looked shattered. Janine knew the feeling.

'In some ways they need you more,' she said, 'Tom especially—'

'Janine,' he interrupted her, 'Tina's got post-natal depression.' He looked at her, then away. Was he serious? She saw him swallow, the slump of his shoulders as he exhaled.

'She can't get out of bed half the time. She can't even feed him. It's all I can do to keep turning up for my shifts and look after her and the baby. We're really struggling.'

'Oh God, Pete.' She stared at him for a moment, taking it in. 'Has she seen a doctor?'

'Yeah,' he said, 'be a while till the medication kicks in.' He sounded defeated. Janine had come across women suffering from the condition over the years, even one of them through work, a case of infanticide. Heart breaking. She could barely imagine the enormous strain of dealing with the illness alongside the demands of a new baby.

'You should have told me,' Janine said, 'why didn't you say anything sooner?'

He shrugged, 'Hoped she'd improve.' She felt sorry for him, a novel experience. She knew the baby had not been part of Pete's game plan, as he put it. When he moved in with Tina he'd been hoping for a different life, unencumbered by kids and their demands. Now here he was starting out on parenthood all over again.

'Right,' Janine said, 'I'll explain to the kids. At least they won't think you've traded them in for a younger model.'

He shot her a look.

'You want a drink?' Janine said.

He gave a wry smile. 'I'd love a drink.'

They chatted over a glass of wine, Janine filling him in on Eleanor's current mood and Charlotte's antics. He promised that once things were on an even keel he'd be back on his regular visits.

'You can always bring him here,' Janine said, surprising herself, 'bring him with you, if Tina's OK to be left.'

'That's not a bad idea.'

'I'm sure Tom would love to teach him the finer points of Call of Duty or whatever,' Janine said.

Pete laughed.

She felt a moment's poignancy, missing this, the company, the shared humour though after four years she was used to dealing with the kids, with the house, on her own.

And it seemed to be all she could fit in her life. No space for romance. There were times when it looked like Richard and she might rekindle the flame that had flared between them briefly at the start of their careers, but she'd stepped back from the brink, realising she would rather have the certainty of his friendship than a risky shot at being a couple. And Richard's track record with women wasn't particularly persuasive if she was honest, he liked pastures new. Best all round, she thought as she saw Pete out, single, celibate, shattered.

CHAPTER 41

Day Five — Saturday

'The gun is still the only hard evidence we've got. Aaron Matthews fired it two years ago — and got sent down. The weapon was never recovered. And there's no record of it being used in any crime since . . . until this week. Follow the gun,' Janine said.

'Boss, when we were in the car,' Lisa said, 'he claimed he sold it. Maybe he did.'

Shap shook his head. 'Nah! One of the gang-banger's been looking after the gun for him while he's inside, out he comes, gets it back, they have another go at the surgery and bang, bang, back on form. Friends reunited.'

'Maybe,' Janine said.

'We could offer a reward: information leading to conviction,' Butchers said.

'Not yet,' Janine said, 'let's have another go at Matthews.'

'We can't arrest him,' Richard said.

'I'm not suggesting that,' Janine said, 'we talk to him, nicely, see if he'll tell us who he sold the gun to. Lisa, Shap, see if he'll co-operate?'

'What's the point?' Shap said.

'If you don't ask . . .' Janine said. OK it was a long shot. Matthews, protesting his innocence, was going to stay as far away from them as possible. Richard was right, they hadn't got any new evidence to justify arresting him for interview. Picking him up might be construed as harassment and she didn't want the investigation undermined by allegations like that. So a long shot it would have to be.

* * *

There was no answer from Aaron Matthews' flat. Lisa wondered if he'd left town. If they were too late. Shap knocked again, long and loud. 'Come on, Mr Matthews, we know you're there.'

'Piss off,' came from inside.

'Have you told your probation officer about our interest?' Shap said, 'Your licence can be revoked, can't it, for any infringement. Resisting arrest, for example, they'd whip you back inside before you could fasten your flies . . .' Always ready with a threat, Shap was, he liked to apply pressure at the slightest opportunity. It was not a very attractive quality, Lisa thought. And it was not what the boss had asked them to do.

The door opened. Aaron Matthews could barely stand, he was bent over in pain. There was blood on his T-shirt, gashes on his face, one eye swollen shut, he held his hand as though it was broken. From his posture Lisa suspected some broken ribs too.

'Jesus,' she said, 'what happened?'

'You happened,' Matthews said, hobbling into the flat, 'and word got back. You satisfied?' Angry words but his voice was close to breaking.

'You should go to hospital,' Lisa said, closing the door. 'Sarge,' she said, 'I think we should get a paramedic to see him.'

Matthews shook his head.

'You'll have a drink of water?' Lisa said. She turned to Shap who did his mock outrage look at being asked to do anything he thought she — as a junior, as a woman — should be doing. Lisa held her nerve. No way would Aaron talk with Shap playing the heavy but just maybe he'd talk to Lisa. Shap rolled his eyes and sighed and went out to the kitchen.

'Who did this to you?' Lisa said quietly.

'Guess,' Aaron said.

'The Wilson Crew? But why, you didn't tell us anything.'

'You think they care?' Matthews said. 'Just being seen with you lot, picked up and released, that's all it takes. I get warned and everyone gets the message.'

'You could press charges,' Lisa said.

Aaron started to laugh, no humour there, but winced and stopped. 'And end up a dead man?' he said.

'Have you ever thought about witness protection?' Lisa said.

'No way,' he said, 'then they would kill me.'

'They'd have to find you first,' Lisa said, 'we're very good at hiding people.'

Shap came back in with the water but held onto it and said, 'This gun you allegedly sold, before you went inside, who'd you flog it to?'

Aaron stared at him. 'You're joking, aren't you?'

'Was it another crew member, eh? The Wilson gang were behind the first robbery at the medical centre. Did some of them go back for more this week, take your gun along?'

'I don't know,' Aaron said with heavy emphasis. 'And even if I did, I'm not a snitch. But hey, they think I am — so what's the point, eh?' He spread his hands, palms up, imploring.

'Why not give it up?' Lisa saw tears in his eyes, he blinked them away, his face was mobile, rage flickering across it.

'I didn't sell it to any of them, right? It was a lad from the Wilbraham Estate. Carter, he called himself, he used to buy his stash from us.'

Lisa felt adrenalin sting through her veins. They had a lead.

'First name?' Shap said.

'Dunno,' Matthews said, the outburst over.

'How old?' Shap said.

'Seventeen, eighteen?' Matthews gave a shrug. 'Not seen him since.'

'And that was before you went down?' Shap said.

'Yes. Now piss off and leave us alone.'

Shap was gloating as they went down the steps at the side of the maisonettes. 'You were hoping a bit of tea and sympathy and he'd do a Jerry Springer for you, weren't you? Tell all and then you could clean your copybook. Scallies like that, you've got to go in hard. Keep the pressure on. Now,' he turned back to face her, triumphant, 'now, we've got a name.'

CHAPTER 42

The incident boards now excluded both Neil Langan and Norma Halliwell as suspects. New information on Norma and the theft of drugs by Halliwell was noted. And the name Carter had been added. As of yet, that, and a guess at his age, was all they had but the team were busy trying to find out just who had bought the gun from Aaron Matthews.

Shap was scanning Electoral Records online. Lisa was looking at local birth records. She had described Aaron Matthews' situation to Janine when they arrived back.

'He's in a right mess,' Lisa said, 'taken a right beating.'

'It looks worse than it is,' Shap said.

'Poor sod,' Janine said, 'he couldn't win, could he. What choices did he have? Join the gang or else. Then when he tries to break away, he loses everything. Gets leathered into the bargain. They don't trust him, we don't trust him.'

'It could have something to do with his taste for violent crime and drug dealing,' Richard said.

'There's this concept called rehabilitation,' Janine said, 'heard of it?'

Now Shap called out, 'No male called Carter, of that age, on the current Electoral roll for the ward.'

'South Manchester, there's a Carter, Simon, in the birth records, July 87,' Lisa said, 'looks good.'

A few moments later Shap said, 'Previous year, on the electoral roll, we've a Margaret Carter, that could be the mother, and that's on the Wilbraham Estate.'

'Nice one,' Richard said. Janine felt excitement gathering as things fell into place. Please, she hoped, let this be a firm lead. 'It looks like Matthews could be telling the truth, after all.'

Lisa glanced at her, no doubt very relieved that Aaron Matthews was no longer a suspect.

Butchers came in, picked up on the hubbub and scanned the boards.

'What's going on?' he said.

'Progress,' Shap said. 'While you've been sitting on your arse, we've been busy — lad called Simon Carter, could be our shooter.'

'Aaron Matthews sold him the gun,' Lisa said, 'he was living on the Wilbraham estate.'

'Carter?' Butchers frowned. 'Hang on. . .' Butchers pulled out his notebook, flipped through it. 'Here we are,' he said, 'Simon Carter.'

'Patient with a grudge?' Richard guessed, 'There's our motive. Means and motive. I knew it!'

'No,' Butchers said, 'he's not a complainant, he's an ex-patient. As in deceased.' He looked at Janine. 'You asked me to find all the people who'd left the practice. Well — some of them have died.'

Janine felt the hope deflate, yet another false lead, a flaming cul-de-sac.

'Simon Carter died two years ago,' Butchers said.

'Not long after Matthews had sold him the gun,' Shap said.

'And dead men don't shoot guns,' Janine said.

'Well, Carter must have given the gun to someone else, then,' Richard said.

'Christ!' said Janine, 'it's like bloody pass-the-parcel.' Frustration made her chest tight. She addressed the team,

'Dig up everything on Simon Carter. Was he in one of the gangs? Who else did he know — the gun may have gone to an associate? Can we trace the family, are they still at the Wilbraham Estate house? What did he die of? Was he shot?' She asked Butchers the last question but Butchers looked blank.

'No bells ringing?' Janine said, 'No light-bulb moment?'

'He uses low energy, boss,' Shap said, 'ten minutes to warm up and you still can't see anything.'

'Funny. Not,' Janine said. 'Can we get hold of the death certificate?

'I'll try the schools for Carter, boss,' Lisa said.

'Butchers — try calling the house, Carter's last known residence,' Janine said.

They hit the phones.

So near and yet so far, Janine thought. What had Simon Carter done with the gun? If they could just find that out.

'Sarge,' Lisa called to Shap, 'you're wanted in reception.'

* * *

Aaron Matthews was waiting for Shap.

'What?' Shap said.

The lad dithered, on the brink, not actually saying anything. Looked down at the carpet.

'Someone nicked your bike?' Shap said

'I want to talk to someone about witness protection,' Matthews said. 'There's stuff I know, going back a bit. But I'd need a new place, like, a new name and everything.' Shap couldn't believe what he was hearing. 'You sure about that?' he said.

'Yeah. I've no life here, have I?' Matthews looked away from him, his jaw working.

'Right,' Shap said, 'come this way.' That sort of information could eviscerate the Wilson Crew, Shap thought, take them out of circulation for good. Did the lad have any idea of what he was letting himself in for? Cut off from everything he'd ever known, he'd have to leave the city and never return. Shap wasn't about to enlighten him; scally might change his mind and that would be a great pity.

* * *

Richard printed off copies of the birth and death certificates for Simon Carter.

The team gathered round as he read aloud, 'Cause of death: multiple injuries. Person reporting the death — Roy Gant, father.'

Silence fell in the room. *Roy Gant?* 'What?' Janine said.

Richard read out the birth certificate. 'Simon Carter: mother Margaret Carter, clerical worker, father Roy Gant, warehouse manager.'

'Fuck me,' said Shap.

'Margaret Carter, known as Peggy Gant,' Butchers said and began typing. 'She's the one who just died.'

'What's with the names?' Janine said.

'Catholics,' Butchers said, 'can't divorce, one of them must have been married before.'

'Check that,' Janine said. 'And Simon was their son. Multiple injuries, what's that mean? Car crash? Shooting? Was there any foul play? Lisa find out more about how Simon Carter died.'

Roy Gant, what had they missed? Dr Halliwell had seen Gant on the Tuesday lunchtime when the GP certified Peggy's death. Janine recalled the man, vaguely, returning the oxygen canister on the Wednesday, swapping condolences with Ms Ling.

'Got it, boss,' Lisa shouted, 'Newspaper reports.'

Janine bent over Lisa's shoulder and read the headline: *TRAGIC TEEN SUICIDE ON M60.*

'You remember this?' Janine said to the others. Richard nodded.

'Jumped off a motorway bridge,' Shap said.

Lisa scrolled down, clicked on a second website, showing pictures of Simon and his parents, Roy and Peggy Gant.

Janine scanned the text, *Being treated for depression by his GP.* 'Oh, Christ,' she said.

* * *

Janine rattled through what they now knew. 'Simon Carter is depressed, Dr Halliwell prescribes for him, and soon after the boy kills himself. But the Gants never complain. Peggy's already ill, she has a bad heart and emphysema and Simon's death makes it worse. They move house, Peggy deteriorates. Gant nurses her. Then she dies. Gant's on his own. He's lost them both.'

'He blames Halliwell,' Richard said.

'Gant had Simon's gun, he must have kept it after Simon died,' Janine said. 'We bring him in now. You three,' she gestured to Richard, Shap and Butchers, 'set off. We'll co-ordinate armed response, get them to rendezvous with you at Gant's, then we'll follow on.'

CHAPTER 43

Armed police were in position near to the house, and the area was already cordoned off, as Richard, Shap and Butchers emerged from their cars. One good thing you could say about the terrorist threat, Shap thought, people got their shit together far quicker these days.

'Any sign of him?' Richard asked the leader of the armed unit.

'No. We'll go in.'

Richard nodded.

The armed police moved into position and the pair at the front used a battering ram to break into the house. It only took two blows and the door swung open.

'Clear.'

'Clear.'

The shouts and the drumming of boots on the stairs came as the unit checked each room.

The leader of the armed unit came outside to them, then. 'No one present.'

'Thank you,' Richard said, 'we'll take it from here.'

He turned to Shap and Butchers. 'See if the neighbours know anything, I'll start looking for the gun.'

Richard pulled on latex gloves. The living room was bare looking, almost monastic. Richard went through to the kitchen, it had an abandoned feel but it was tidy. He looked in the fridge and it was empty. Completely empty. Who had an empty fridge? Richard opened the back door and looked in the wheelie bin, it was almost full. On top of the rubbish were a tomato sauce bottle, a pack of butter and half a loaf of bread.

* * *

Shap struck lucky at the first house. 'He's not here,' the neighbour said, 'he's at his wife's funeral. The car left a couple of hours ago.'

'Where's the funeral?' Shap said.

'Southern Cemetery,' she said.

Shap told Richard who rang and told the boss. The boss said she and Lisa would go to the cemetery and see if Gant was still there while the others continued the search for the weapon. It's crucial, the boss told them, no gun and I'm not sure we can make a case.

* * *

On the way to the cemetery, Janine waited for word back from Richard that they had found the gun. She feared that Roy Gant might elude them. The case had been one lead after another turning to disappointment: Fraser McKee, Aaron Matthews, Neil Langan, Norma and now Gant. Was he really the one? Or would he turn out to be just like all the other suspects? It was like studying pictures made of sand, which disappeared when the wind changed direction. But this time it did all add up, she told herself, it did. And she pressed the accelerator down even further.

CHAPTER 44

There were so many questions. Norma sat in an anteroom with a psychiatric social worker who went through the forms. Evaluation. Risk assessment. Care package. There was talk of a rehabilitation programme. Perhaps some people did turn their lives around, make a fresh start. For her it seemed like a fantasy. What would she do with her life? Even if she battled the addiction and won, her only work experience was teaching piano. Money wasn't an issue, anyway, the mortgage was paid off and Don had life insurance. She'd be able to manage. And what was the point, really? There was no hunger in her for anything but oblivion. She'd no close friends or family to cheer her on. The pit was waiting, wider and deeper than ever.

'Have you had any suicidal thoughts in the past twenty-four hours?' the woman said.

Too harsh, that word, it made Norma recoil. All she wanted to do was sleep, sleep and not wake. Already her skin was itchy and her stomach cramping. She felt wild and anxious. One of the nurses said she'd be able to have some medication for the symptoms only after she'd been evaluated. Without Don, without the medicine, what was there to live for?

'Sometimes,' Norma said.

The social worker made a tick on the form. 'Have you made any attempt to act on these thoughts?'

'My husband has just died,' Norma said, suddenly sick of it all, cross with the way they were treating her.

'I know. I am sorry,' the social worker said, 'this must be very, very difficult for you. But we need to go through this so we can get you in the system, access services to help you.'

Norma didn't want to be in the system, she didn't want to be here at all. Lonely, widowed, sixty-two years old. Yes, people built new lives, like the police inspector had said, they joined clubs or volunteered, they lunched and golfed and started charities. Other people. Not her. She'd never been a joiner, never had any interest.

She wanted to go back, to the woods in France and the time when Pierre played the harmonica, and kissed her neck. When life lay ahead like a promise, or before the baby when she and Don were giddy with love and punch drunk from studying and working. He would test her at the breakfast table, regions of the brain or indications of pulmonary heart disease.

She wanted to go back, not forward.

The woman repeated the question. 'No,' Norma said, 'no attempts.'

And there was no chance in here. The medicines came round in the trolley, two nurses carefully unlocked it and measured and ticked off what was dispensed.

The social worker carried on. Norma answered the questions, she had to because the hunger was growing and she was more and more desperate, her throat dry and tight, her vision pitching and blurring. She must do as they said to get the methadone or whatever they would put her on. For now that was all that mattered.

CHAPTER 45

When Howard came into the living room, Adele had all the papers from the inquest and all the cuttings from the papers strewn around on the couch and the coffee table.

The laptop was on her knee and she was copying something onto a pad of paper.

'What're you doing?' Howard said.

'Research,' Adele said. She tapped her pen on the pad. 'All the groups who are campaigning for a change to the drugs law.'

'Seriously?'

She turned to him. 'You think I should just give up now, because Halliwell's dead?'

'You're exhausted,' he said, 'and all this. . .' He waved his hand across the papers.

'This keeps me going,' she said, 'I'm doing it for Marcie, for all the others who end up shooting up in some rat hole because they're treated as criminals not patients. Because the politicians decide that they'll win votes if they keep banging on about a war on drugs. Never mind that it doesn't work.'

'You don't need to tell me,' Howard said.

'There's people talking about a return to the English system,' she said, 'when addicts were registered and managed by the doctor, they weren't forced onto other drugs or weaned off stuff too quickly. They lived with the addiction, safely. It worked. They weren't out robbing and mugging people to buy drugs. In Portugal they've legalised drugs, all drugs, ten years it's been like that and addiction rates have fallen.' Adele realised her voice had risen and Howard was looking at her with a half-smile on his lips.

'You go girl,' he said.

'You watch me,' she said.

CHAPTER 46

The wind was cold, coming from the east. It made his eyes water. The priest finished the final prayer and sprinkled more holy water down onto the coffin. There had been a fantastic turnout at the mass and maybe half had come on for the burial. The programme made it clear that there'd be no gathering afterwards. It had all happened so quickly that people probably imagined Roy hadn't been able to hire a venue, though the church hall might have been available at short notice. Anyway there would be no tea and finger buffet, no sherry and swapping of shared memories and words of comfort.

He took the box of earth and picked up a handful, let it fall into the grave, and passed the box on. When everyone had taken their turn, the priest blessed them and sent them on their way.

People came to him, taking leave, hands grasping his, or touching his arm. Finally the priest left and Roy stood alone.

He saw the cars arrive, sensed they were here for him, surprised, if he were honest, that they had put it all together so quickly. He hadn't wanted witnesses. If they'd only taken half an hour longer. No one should have to witness this.

When Simon died, when the police come with that dreadful news, Roy had felt anger and grief, but more than that he felt awash with guilt. Because he'd not fought harder for his son, because when he challenged Don Halliwell about the treatment, about the known dangers of that medication and Halliwell had dismissed him, Roy had not done more.

Peggy hated the strife between them. 'He's a doctor, Roy, we have to trust him.' Even when Roy had shown her the evidence, the headlines, the cries for reclassification, the stories of teenagers made even more sick by this very same medicine, Peggy had said, 'Well, he knows now, and if he thinks it's not working, surely he'll change it.'

But he wouldn't, Roy realized when it was too late. He wouldn't because the man was stubborn and arrogant and he would rather sacrifice a child's life than admit he was fallible.

It had just happened again with Adele Young's daughter. The man had learned nothing. What good were complaints procedures and inquests in the light of such a wilful disregard for other opinions?

Halliwell would not listen, he would not learn. He set himself up as being above all that. Better than his patients. Always right. And he never said sorry, not once in all the horror of Simon's death had Halliwell ever taken them aside or stopped for a moment to say, I am sorry, you tried to tell me.

He accepted not one shred of responsibility but acted as though Simon's desperation, his paranoia, his desire to die, to escape it all, was some force of nature. Random and inexplicable. Not directly linked to the drug he prescribed. Never mind the fact that Roy had run himself ragged before it happened trying to get Halliwell just to look at the studies, begging him to consider the concerns, warning him that lives had been lost.

Halliwell had fobbed Roy off and sent him home where a look at Peggy's face confirmed his fears. Simon was worse.

Now at the cemetery, a gust of wind blew and Roy felt it cold against the back of his neck, on his ears, nipping at his shins.

That last time, after Halliwell had almost lost his temper, snapping, 'For God's sake, Roy, we've been over this.

I'm Simon's doctor. There is frequently a period of adjustment and if things have not levelled out in another week I will be happy to review the prescription then. Now, please, I have work to do.' Roy saw that Halliwell was immovable. Roy could not bear the prospect of another week with Simon living in terror, seeing demons and hearing voices, rocking and sobbing. Simon, so scared that he bought a gun. It was a situation, a world, that Roy could barely comprehend. His boy with a gun in his bedroom. What would he shoot with it? The monsters that his illness had conjured up?

Roy found it by accident when Simon was in the bathroom. Peggy had been persuading him to have a shower or at least a wash. Simon said he couldn't. He asked Roy to cover the mirror up. Roy was exasperated. What should he do? If he went along with this latest delusion, would he be reinforcing it? Should he refuse, insist that there was nothing sinister in the mirror, or behind the shower curtain? In the end he ran some hot water, so the steam covered the glass.

'It's all right, Simon,' he said, 'you'll be all right. I'll just be here, I'll wait here.'

'But Dad—'

'Go on now. You'll feel better for a wash.'

The boy smelled of sweat and tobacco. His hair was messy, his face angry with spots. Simon had gone into the bathroom and Roy went to change his bed and found the gun under his pillow. He felt a shock, like a blow to the heart, as he saw it and understood that it was real, that his son had brought a gun into the house. Roy picked it up. It was heavy, cold to touch, hard. Roy had never seen a gun close up before. He wrapped it in a small towel and put it on top of the wardrobe in his and Peggy's bedroom. Then he stripped Simon's bed and made it up new.

He went to the bathroom and knocked and passed Simon some clean jeans and underwear and a T-shirt.

Roy sat on the edge of the bed and waited. He could hear water running in the sink, and Peggy moving about downstairs. When Simon came back in, shivering, his arms thin sticks poking out of the T-shirt, Roy patted the bed beside him. 'Sit down.'

Simon did.

'I found the gun,' Roy said.

'What?' Simon looked alarmed.

'I put it somewhere safe,' Roy said.

'I need it.'

'No. You'll hurt yourself or someone else.'

'You don't get it, do you?' Simon said, his voice louder, eyes frantic, 'You don't understand.'

'I know this is hard,' Roy said.

Simon was crying again.

Roy moved to put an arm around him, miserable himself.

'Don't!' Simon flinched away.

'Your mum and I—'

'Just go. Leave me alone.' Simon's knee was jerking up and down, a measure of the anxiety.

'Simon?'

'Go away!'

Roy sighed and got to his feet. He thought about telling Simon what the doctor had said, that another week might see a change in his mood and they could try another drug if not. Was that offering false hope? Roy didn't believe things would improve. Should he tell Simon what he thought they should do in the meanwhile?

He said nothing.

Peggy was in the kitchen, chopping vegetables. The washing machine was on, the spin part of the cycle, deafening. She looked at Roy, eyes busy with questions and gestured for him to come in the other room to talk. When he told her about the gun she lost her breath and had to use her inhaler.

'Listen,' he said as soon as her breathing had eased, 'I've had an idea. Dr Halliwell wants to leave it another week. I don't think — look, we could see about getting him in somewhere.'

'Mental hospital? How?'

'I don't know, but I can find out.' Did you call the police or an ambulance? He feared it would need a referral from Simon's own GP. 'If it was an emergency,' Roy said, 'which it is . . .'

'Have him committed, sectioned?' Peggy said.

Roy took her hand. 'He's not safe,' he said, 'he's getting worse, Peggy.'

'I don't know,' Peggy said.

'We've got to do something,' Roy said, 'even if Don Halliwell won't.'

Peggy frowned, she didn't like it when he criticized the doctor. Roy wondered why, when she stood up against the rules and regulations or her religion in order to be with him, to have a family, then why did she still kowtow to the GP?

'I'll find out,' Roy said, 'somewhere like that, they must deal with this sort of thing all the time, they're specialists.'

She gave a nod, eyes riddled with worry.

* * *

'Mr Gant, Roy?' They were here for him now. The police.

Roy looked down at the grave, the artificial grass. Down the hill he saw movement, two men smoking, rough clothes, spades leaning against a tree. The grave diggers waiting for him to leave.

CHAPTER 47

Shap came downstairs holding up Dr Halliwell's briefcase. 'I don't think we'll need the gun if we've got this,' he said.

'Why keep the briefcase?' Richard said, 'Why didn't he get rid of it?'

'Thick?' Shap said.

'It would be watertight if we had the gun as well,' Richard said, 'keep looking. I'll ring Janine and tell her we've got the briefcase.'

* * *

It was a cold, blustery, miserable day for a funeral, or maybe an appropriate one.

Janine parked some distance from the crematorium, eyes roving over the grounds. She saw the group of mourners drifting away from a graveside down the hill.

'I don't think there's anything in the PACE rules says at what point you interrupt a funeral,' Janine said, getting out of the car.

'Looks like they're done,' Lisa said.

Still no word from Richard but Janine reckoned they had enough to question Gant while the search for the weapon continued. She saw Gant look up and notice them but he stayed by the grave.

They walked along the path and down the slope to the freshly dug plot. The priest took his leave and once he had moved far enough away to be out of earshot Janine spoke to Roy Gant. 'Mr Gant, Roy.'

* * *

Roy had been too late in the end. He'd rung round helpline numbers in the phone directory. Most of them told him the GP should set an emergency admission in motion; failing that he could ring the local social services. A mental health social worker working with the police could arrange a section.

He explained to Peggy. 'I don't know,' she said, 'I just don't know.'

Roy had gone upstairs to tell Simon his tea was ready, would he come and have some, to find his bedroom deserted.

He had driven round with no idea where to look. Simon had not wanted to leave the house recently, the outside world as scary as the one in his head.

Roy went home when it got dark. Peggy had reported him missing and as he was known to be vulnerable the local police were alerted to be on the lookout for him.

Roy hadn't been back ten minutes when they had come to the door, a man and a woman, very serious and ill at ease. They asked Peggy and him to sit down and Roy felt dread scrabble up his spine, clutch at his guts. The woman spoke, 'A young man matching Simon's description was involved in an accident earlier this evening. I'm afraid he didn't survive his injuries.'

'Simon,' Peggy said. She began to gasp for air. Roy passed her inhaler, helped her to use it.

'What accident?' Roy said, clasping Peggy's hand. The words hurt his throat.

'A fall from a motorway bridge.'

'He didn't fall,' Roy said.

Peggy's breathing worsened.

'Mrs Gant?' said the police officer.

'You'd better get an ambulance for her,' Roy had said.

Now someone else was calling him. 'Mr Gant?'

Roy turned away from the grave.

'Leave me,' he said, 'please?'

It wasn't meant to be like this, they were too soon.

* * *

'I can't do that. I'm DCI Lewis, I'm investigating the murder of Dr Halliwell. I'm sorry to intrude on your grief but we're going to need you to come with us.' Then she began the caution.

'Roy Gant, I am arresting you on suspicion of murder. You do not have to say anything—'

'He never listened,' Roy Gant interrupted, not looking at Janine but staring down at the coffin, the wind snatching at his clothes. 'There was stuff all over the internet, I printed it off, I showed him. Increased risk of suicide in young people . . . messing with drugs was what made Simon depressed in the first place. When he started the tablets . . .'

'You might want to wait until you've seen a solicitor,' Janine said.

Roy Gant dismissed her concern with a toss of his head. 'He didn't even read the damn journals. If he'd ever said, "Sorry, I got it wrong—"' He broke off. He rubbed his fist on his forehead. 'Simon was my world, and then he was gone.'

'And Peggy?' Janine said.

'She wouldn't hear a bad word said about the man. She was there when I begged Halliwell to come and see Simon for himself. "Give it time," he said. We didn't have time. How she trusted him, Peggy. All the way to the motorway bridge, still following doctor's orders.'

'You never made a complaint?' Janine said.

'Peggy was so sick, I couldn't make it worse for her,' Roy Gant said. 'The doctor would call round with his smiles and

169

his crumbs of comfort.' He glanced at Janine, eyes narrowed. 'You heard about Marcie Young?'

Janine nodded.

'He'd learnt nothing,' Gant said. 'He still didn't listen. Masking his ignorance with arrogance.'

'Why now, Roy?' Janine said.

'He came on Tuesday, after Peggy had gone. You know what he said? "It'll get easier, Roy. Life goes on." Smug bastard. His life would,' Gant said. '*They* were my life. I knew then.'

'You had Simon's gun?' Janine said.

'"I took it off him.' Roy Gant hesitated, blinked several times.

'Why did Simon have a gun in the first place?' Janine said.

'He was petrified. He thought it would protect him. How can you protect yourself when the demons are inside?' Gant's voice broke. Janine waited and eventually he cleared his throat and said, 'The demons grew with that drug, they fed on it. But Halliwell was blind and deaf and dumb to it.' Roy Gant shifted, looked up to the sky. 'He was usually the last to leave the surgery,' he said, 'so I went down there. It was easy.'

'You took his briefcase?' Janine said.

'Yes, well, children might have found it, taken stuff and hurt themselves,' he said.

Oh God. 'And where did you put the gun?' Janine said.

He moved then, his face set as he pulled the gun from his pocket and pointed it at them. Janine's heart leapt into her throat. She felt sick inside. She heard Lisa take a quick breath and Janine put out a hand, instinctively, to prevent Lisa moving towards Gant.

'Stay there!' Roy Gant said and he began to back away, across the grass, gun trained on them all the while.

Janine's mouth was dry, her pulse racing. He wouldn't get far, she told herself, even if he did shoot at them, the whole force would be out after him in minutes. Same if he fled.

She watched, her legs like jelly, as he reached a stand of trees, dark green yews, their branches shivering in the wind.

Beside her Lisa was gasping, whispering, 'Oh, God, oh God, no.'

Would he hit them from this distance? Janine thought of Charlotte, of Tom and Eleanor, of Michael and clamped her mouth tight, determined to keep watching, not to close her eyes.

'Roy, wait,' she called out but the wind seemed to rip her words away. 'Roy, we can talk about this, about Simon, and Marcie Young, you could help her family—'

He turned quickly, facing the trees and raised the gun to his head.

'No!' Janine screamed and Lisa echoed her.

The shot, a crack of thunder, echoed round the cemetery.

'No!' Janine yelled as the blood and brain burst from his head and he pitched forward onto his knees and then onto his face.

Birds rose screeching from the trees. Lisa was howling and Janine grabbed her, held her, turning her away.

'Come on,' Janine said, 'this way. Come on.'

Shaking violently, Janine thought she would collapse, but she walked with Lisa up to the car, aware of the gravediggers shouting, and someone running and the starlings crying as they wheeled overhead.

Janine called it in.

And then she sat with Lisa in the car, waiting for the police and the ambulance. Waiting to give a witness statement. Waiting until she could go home and see her kids and try to forget the image strobing in her mind, of the heartbroken father with a gun to his head.

CHAPTER 48

It was hours before they were free to go and by that point Janine knew what everyone needed was some rest and relaxation, to debrief with those who had shared the experience. Pete had the kids and had promised to be back for half eight. She must be home by then so she had invited the team back to hers for pizza and beer.

Shap was making a good effort to get everyone pissed. He held a bottle out to Janine. 'Have another,' he said, 'doctor's orders.'

'It was personal, after all,' Lisa said quietly.

'It usually is,' Janine said. She caught Lisa's expression, haunted afresh by events.

'We did our best,' Janine said, 'he killed himself, no one else. I wish it hadn't happened but we are not to blame. In that situation there was nothing else we could have done. You must believe that.'

'Something like this,' Richard said to Lisa, 'it stays with you. But you will be all right. If you need some counselling, it's available. It can help.'

'And it's not a sign of weakness,' Janine said.

Lisa gave a ghost of a smile.

Butchers handed out pizza. 'Taking orders for deserts,' he said.

'Double chocolate fudge ice-cream,' Lisa said, shaking herself as if waking, and reaching for a big slice of pizza.

A good sign, Janine thought, appetite.

'Where does she put it all?' Richard said.

'Hollow legs,' Janine said.

'Go far with a constitution like that,' Richard said, 'with the right management.'

'Better ask for a transfer then, hadn't I?' Lisa said.

Janine smiled, glad that Richard's rancour had gone, and that Lisa felt secure enough to make banter.

'Try Xcalibre,' Shap put in, 'they're short of a few ladies in waiting.'

'You're not going anywhere,' Richard said, 'the amount of work we've put into you.'

Pete came in, carrying Alfie, Tom and Charlotte following.

'This a private do, or can anyone join in?' Pete said.

'Hello, little one,' Lisa said to the baby.

Alfie burped making everyone laugh.

Janine caught Pete's eyes, shared a look, a mutual, *You OK?* Got a nod in reply. She was, well — she would be. There'd be dreams and moments of sudden fear and sadness. Times when she would torment herself, picking over what she might have done differently, what might have saved Roy Gant and spared Lisa the trauma. There would be flashes of rage too, wild and random, unfocused, but Janine trusted that she'd cope.

She would keep going and learn to live with it. That was her job. Dealing with death, sudden violent death, asking questions, finding answers. That was her job.

She looked across to where Butchers was taking ice-cream requests from the kids and saw Lisa hold her arms out to hold Alfie, saw Shap sneaking out for a fag, Richard watching Janine, giving her a wink, silent support.

All those deaths, Marcie Young, Simon Carter, Don Halliwell, Roy Gant. Lives cut short.

Every day is a gift she thought. Every day. A precious gift.

THE END

ACKNOWLEDGEMENTS

Thanks to everyone involved with *Blue Murder* at Granada and to all the viewers and readers.

ALSO BY CATH STAINCLIFFE

Thank you for reading this book.

If you enjoyed it please leave feedback on Amazon or Goodreads, and if there is anything we missed or you have a question about, then please get in touch. We appreciate you choosing our book.

Founded in 2014 in Shoreditch, London, we at Joffe Books pride ourselves on our history of innovative publishing. We were thrilled to be shortlisted for Independent Publisher of the Year at the British Book Awards.

www.joffebooks.com

We're very grateful to eagle-eyed readers who take the time to contact us. Please send any errors you find to corrections@joffebooks.com. We'll get them fixed ASAP.